Teste Dein Englisch!

Stufe 1

Ein Testbuch für Anfänger

Von
Geoffrey Broughton

Langenscheidt

Berlin München Wien Zürich

Neben den drei Bänden von TESTE DEIN ENGLISCH!
liegt im gleichen Verlag auch der Band
TESTE DEIN BUSINESS ENGLISH! vor
(ISBN 3-468-38503-X).
Mit diesem Band können Sie Ihre Kenntnisse in der
englischen Wirtschaftssprache verbessern.

Auflage:	8. 7.	|	Letzte Zahlen
Jahr:	1984	|	maßgeblich

Originalausgabe: "Know Your English", Hutchinson & Co
(Publishers) Ltd, London

Zeichnungen: Joseph Wright
Umschlagentwurf: grafik-dienst
Druck: Pressedruck, Augsburg
Printed in Germany · ISBN 3-468-38500-5

Zur Einführung

Alle Anfänger und viele Fortgeschrittene machen Fehler, die ihre englischsprechenden Partner als merkwürdig, komisch oder peinlich empfinden. Sie gebrauchen das falsche Wort, die falsche Wendung, eine falsche grammatische Form oder eine unkorrekte Aussprache. Mit TESTE DEIN ENGLISCH! bekommt der Englischlernende solche Dinge in den Griff. Seine Englischkenntnisse werden durch Abtesten systematisch aufgebaut.

Das Testprinzip dieses Buches ist das „Multiple-choice-Verfahren", d. h. nach jeder in Englisch gestellten Frage werden dem Lernenden 5 Antworten zur Auswahl angeboten, von denen er eine als die richtige Lösung kennzeichnen muß. Durch Umblättern zu den „Answers" kann er sich dann selbst kontrollieren; er findet dort auch die Begründung für die richtige Lösung sowie weitere Erläuterungen zum Fragenkomplex.

Diese Methode unterscheidet sich von den herkömmlichen Lernformen. Sie ist anregend, oft amüsant. Die Kürze der Lerneinheit – die Frage – ermöglicht ein zwangloses Arbeiten auch unterwegs oder wenn wenig Zeit zur Verfügung steht.

Trotzdem basiert die Methode auf modernen linguistischen Erkenntnissen. Dafür bürgt schon der Name des Autors. Geoffrey Broughton ist Leiter des „Department of English as a Foreign Language" an der Londoner Universität. Seine erfolgreichen Lehrbücher sind in der ganzen Welt verbreitet. Aus eigener Praxis kennt er die Fallen, welche die englische Sprache für den Lernenden bereithält.

Die Serie TESTE DEIN ENGLISCH! umfaßt drei Bände, die nach Schwierigkeitsstufen gegliedert sind:

Stufe 1 – ein Testbuch für Anfänger
Stufe 2 – ein Testbuch für Fortgeschrittene
Stufe 3 – ein Testbuch für Könner

Wenn Sie nur geringe Englischkenntnisse haben, beginnen Sie mit dem Band der Stufe 1. Stufe 2 ist für denjenigen gedacht, der schon einige Jahre Englisch gelernt hat. Falls Sie sich aber als „Könner" betrachten, dann zeigt Ihnen Stufe 3, daß es auch für Sie noch einige „harte Nüsse" gibt.

So arbeiten Sie mit diesem Buch

- Nach dem Lesen jeder Frage prüfen Sie bitte sorgfältig, welche der nachgestellten 5 Antworten (a–e) die richtige Lösung darstellt.

- Wenn Sie die richtige Antwort gefunden haben, schreiben Sie den entsprechenden Buchstaben (a, b, c, d, e) in das Kästchen am Rand.

- Haben Sie eine Unit durchgearbeitet, so schlagen Sie die „Answers" auf. Prüfen Sie jetzt, ob Ihre Antworten richtig waren, und studieren Sie die Erläuterungen zu den Fragenkomplexen.

- Ermitteln Sie die Anzahl Ihrer richtigen Antworten und tragen Sie das Ergebnis in das Kästchen für die betreffende Unit auf der Seite „Ihr Testergebnis" ein.

- Auf den Seiten „Wie geht es weiter?" am Ende von Teil A und B werden Ihre Testergebnisse ausgewertet und danach die Weichen für Ihre weitere Arbeit gestellt.

- Das INHALTSVERZEICHNIS finden Sie auf Seite 208.

TEIL A

Unit one

1 Which of these means *at once*?
   a. shortly
   b. later
   c. immediately
   d. at present
   e. soon

2 Which is the correct order of size?
   a. string, cotton, rope
   b. string, rope, cotton
   c. rope, cotton, string
   d. cotton, string, rope
   e. cotton, rope, string

3 Which is wrong?
   a. Don't catch a cold.
   b. I think I am catching a cold.
   c. You have catched a cold.
   d. She often catches colds.
   e. He has caught a cold.

4 This man has got
   a. a yellow eye
   b. a black eye
   c. a green eye
   d. a purple eye
   e. a blue eye

5 What is the opposite of *more*?
a. few
b. less
c. many
d. a lot
e. a little

6 We talk about one *tooth*, but two
a. teeth
b. tooth
c. tooths
d. tooth's
e. tooths'

7 *Eat* is to *hungry* as *drink* is to
a. hot
b. wet
c. tired
d. thirsty
e. cold

d

8 What is on the house?
a. a door
b. a plane
c. a bird
d. the sky
e. the sun

b

9 Which word does not go with all the others?
a. a net
b. a fish
c. to catch
d. the sea
e. to see

10 Which has a knob?
a. a ceiling
b. a floor
c. a door
d. a window
e. a wall

11 Which of these can you drink?
a. petrol
b. ink
c. paper
d. lemonade
e. ice

12 Which is wrong?
a. He's very sleepable.
b. He wants to sleep.
c. He wants to have a sleep.
d. He looks sleepy.
e. He's sitting there sleepily.

13 Which word does not go with the others?
a. cloudy
b. stormy
c. sunny
d. funny
e. rainy

14 Which two words sound the same?

a. wheel, we'll
b. will, wheel
c. well, will
d. will, we'll
e. we'll, well

15 The opposite of *alive* is

a. asleep
b. ill
c. dead
d. blind
e. quiet

c

16 This is

a. a carrier
b. a bucket
c. a basket
d. a bin
e. a holder

17 Which word does not go with all the others?

a. to teach
b. a train
c. a station
d. rails
e. passengers

a

18 Which answer means nearly the same as *to want*?

a. to ask
b. to need
c. to like
d. to fail
e. to have

19 Which word has a different sound?
- a. fork
- b. walk
- c. work
- d. talk
- e. pork

20 In which sentence does *take off* mean *leave the ground*?
- a. Please take your hand off.
- b. The jet took off on time.
- c. They took 10% off the bill.
- d. He never took his eyes off her.
- e. She took off her shoes.

Unit two

---

1 What is he?
- a. a mechanic
- b. a workman
- c. an assistant
- d. a garage
- e. a driver

2 Which word does not go with all the others?
- a. gardens
- b. flowers
- c. to grow
- d. grass
- e. small

3 *To wink* means
a. to shut and open both eyes quickly
b. to shut and open one eye quickly
c. to shut both eyes
d. to shut one eye
e. to open one eye

4 Which word means *under*?
a. towards
b. above
c. between
d. beneath
e. beside

5 If you call a man Jim, his name is
a. John
b. Jack
c. James
d. Harold
e. Gerald

c

6 Which do we put off?
a. a fire
b. a match
c. a candle
d. an electric light
e. a cigarette lighter

e

7 Which is different?
a. coffee
b. cocoa
c. tea
d. bear
e. beer

d

8 Where is his arm?
a. round her stomach
b. round her side
c. round her waist
d. round her neck
e. round her shoulder

b

9 What is the opposite of *loud*?
a. low
b. silent
c. soft
d. calm
e. noisy

10 Where do you not find a counter?
a. in a shop
b. in a bank
c. in a post office
d. in a telephone kiosk
e. in a library

d

11 Which word has a different sound?
a. height
b. weight
c. eight
d. straight
e. plate

12 Complete this phrase: dustpan and
a. duster
b. mop
c. brush
d. dishcloth
e. sponge

13 What is he doing to the ladder?
a. holding it
b. holding it up
c. lifting it
d. carrying it
e. walking under it

14 What is the opposite of *happy*?
a. glad
b. hard
c. sad
d. heavy
e. dark

15 Which of these is not a piece of furniture?
a. a timetable
b. a bedside table
c. a dining table
d. a coffee table
e. a dressing table

16 Which animal has the longest ears?
a. a cow
b. a horse
c. a mouse
d. a pig
e. a rabbit

17 Which is wrong?
a. Make me laugh.
b. Make some coffee.
c. Make up your mind!
d. I am going to make my hair.
e. Make the beds.

d

18 What is this?
a. a clothes machine
b. a wash machine
c. a washing machine
d. a cleaner
e. a cleaning machine

c

19 Which word means *honest*?
a. truthful
b. good
c. nice
d. sure
e. untrue

20 Which word has the same sound as *tongue*?
a. few
b. long
c. hung
d. vague
e. orange

Unit three

1 Which word describes all the others?
- a. a spinster
- b. a niece
- c. an actress
- d. a female
- e. a nun

2 What is the opposite of *last*?
- a. beginning
- b. end
- c. first
- d. start
- e. finish

3 If you are in an audience, where are you?
- a. in church
- b. in the cinema
- c. at a football match
- d. at home, alone with your records
- e. in a garden, listening to birds

4 Which word has the same sound as *through*?
- a. rough
- b. enough
- c. tough
- d. dug
- e. shoe

5 Where are they sitting?

a. on the table
b. in the table
c. under the table
d. for the table
e. at the table

6 Which word does not go with all the others?

a. a shoe
b. a foot
c. a lace
d. to tie
e. a tie

7 What is this?

a. an iron
b. a smoother
c. a presser
d. a clothes press
e. a press

8 Which is not a vegetable?

a. a cabbage
b. a plum
c. a carrot
d. a cauliflower
e. a beetroot

9 Which of these is not a season of the year?
a. month
b. autumn
c. summer
d. spring
e. winter

10 In which sentence does *pick up* mean *learn*?
a. The car picked up speed.
b. He picked up a little English in London.
c. She fell and picked herself up quickly.
d. I'll pick you up at six o'clock.
e. He picked up his hat and left.

11 Which is wrong?
a. I shall show you the way.
b. I have shown you the way.
c. I shown you the way.
d. I was showing you the way.
e. I must show you the way.

12 Which word has a different sound?
a. might
b. bright
c. write
d. white
e. straight

13 What is he saying?

a. Pick it up!
b. Pick it!
c. Take it up!
d. Take it!
e. Pick up it!

14 Which word does not go with all the others?

a. a dream
b. to sleep
c. a bed
d. a chair
e. night

15 Which word is nearest in meaning to *a stair*?

a. up
b. a step
c. to climb
d. a foot
e. to fall

16 This is

a. a monkey
b. a deer
c. a horse
d. a camel
e. a tiger

17 What is the opposite of *now*?
a. again
b. always
c. then
d. sometimes
e. soon

18 Which means *to collect*?
a. to connect
b. to join
c. to gather
d. to meet
e. to bring

19 If someone says to you: *Keep it under your hat*, what does he mean?
a. You need a haircut.
b. You are bald.
c. He wants you to accept some money.
d. Don't lose your temper!
e. He wants you to keep a secret.

20 If you think something is untrue, you are full of
a. belief
b. believing
c. believable
d. unbelievable
e. disbelief

Unit four

1 Which is not a fruit?
- a. an apple
- b. a pea
- c. an orange
- d. a lemon
- e. a pear

2 Which is wrong?
- a. He's using a walking stick.
- b. He's having a stick.
- c. He's walking with a stick.
- d. He's carrying a walking stick.
- e. He's got a stick in his hand.

3 The opposite of *to buy* is
- a. to sell
- b. to steal
- c. to take
- d. to give
- e. to lend

4 Which word has the same sound as *bowl*?
a. roll
b. howl
c. owl
d. rule
e. fall

5 Which of these has four wheels?
a. a bicycle
b. a moped
c. a scooter
d. a van
e. a motorcycle

6 Which word does not go with all the others?
a. a fly
b. a helicopter
c. a plane
d. an engine
e. to fly

7 This telephone is
a. sounding
b. ringing
c. singing
d. calling
e. speaking

8 Which word does not go with all the others?
a. a dog
b. happy
c. a tail
d. to wag
e. a cat

9 Which of these can you ride?

a. a boat
b. a wolf
c. a train
d. a car
e. a horse

10 Which is wrong?

a. I have lend her money.
b. I am lending her money.
c. I lend her money.
d. I did lend her money.
e. I lent her money.

11 Which word has a different sound?

a. were
b. her
c. sir
d. where
e. fur

12 Which is wrong?

a. I will come with you, as usually.
b. This is not my usual work.
c. Usually, I travel by bus.
d. I missed my usual train.
e. I do not usually go.

13 Two people who are walking along holding hands, are walking

a. hand to hand
b. hand in hand
c. hand against hand
d. hand by hand
e. hand over hand

14 What is he saying?
a. I can't stopped!
b. I can't stopper!
c. I can't stopping!
d. I can't stop!
e. I can't to stop!

d

15 If you call a girl Jenny, her name is
a. Joan
b. Jennifer
c. Jean
d. Janet
e. Joyce

b

16 Which do we not say?
a. a pile of leaves
b. a pile of houses
c. a pile of rubbish
d. a pile of newspapers
e. a pile of old clothes

17 Which means the same as *to answer*?
a. to reply
b. to say
c. to speak
d. to talk
e. to ask

18 Which word describes all the others?

a. a jacket
b. a blouse
c. trousers
d. a skirt
e. clothes

d

19 She is saying: *You didn't use the*

a. bar
b. towel
c. washer
d. cake
e. soap

e

20 The opposite of *good* is

a. bad
b. better
c. worse
d. worst
e. best

a

Unit five

1 Which of these is made of glass?

a. a tumbler
b. teeth
c. sand
d. a knife
e. a cup

2 Which word does not go with all the others?

a. a cold
b. to sneeze
c. a nose
d. hot
e. a handkerchief

3 What is he saying?

a. What's the o'clock?
b. What time is it?
c. What o'clock is it?
d. What hour is it?
e. What's the hour?

4 Which of these is wrong?
a. a clean day
b. a rainy day
c. a fine day
d. a cloudy day
e. a sunny day

5 The opposite of *dangerous* is
a. easy
b. pleasant
c. beautiful
d. comfortable
e. safe

6 Which word does not go with all the others?
a. a letter
b. paper
c. string
d. a parcel
e. to wrap

7 Which word means the same as *also*?
a. all
b. toe
c. to
d. two
e. too

8 Which meat comes from a pig?
a. beef
b. lamb
c. mutton
d. veal
e. bacon

e

9 Which is wrong?
a. There are two books under his arm.
b. Under his arm there are two books.
c. Two books he's got under his arm.
d. He's got two books under his arm.
e. Under his arm he's got two books.

10 What is the answer when someone asks: *Did you bring it?*
a. Yes, I brought it.
b. Yes, I bringed it.
c. Yes, I am broughting it.
d. Yes, I have bring it.
e. Yes, I have broughted it.

a

11 Which is wrong?
a. He explained quickly.
b. He talked aloudly.
c. He laughed noisily.
d. He smiled gently.
e. He slept peacefully.

12 Which of these is longest?

a. a sentence
b. a letter
c. a chapter
d. a paragraph
e. a word

13 Where is the TV?

a. in the corner
b. at the corner
c. on the corner
d. by the corner
e. near the corner

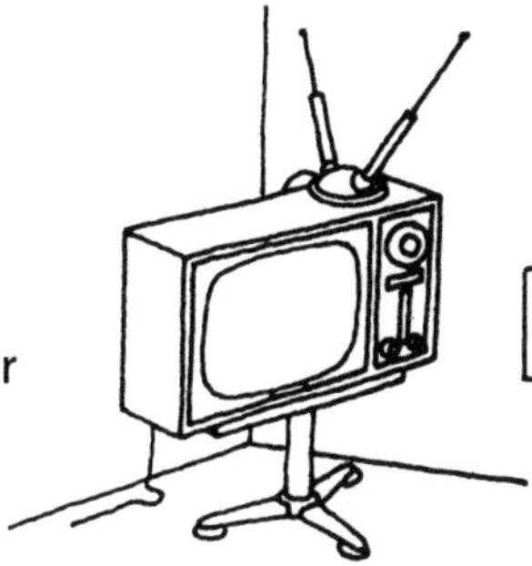

a

14 Where does a porter work?

a. in a church
b. in a supermarket
c. in a library
d. in a railway station
e. in an aeroplane

15 What is a nightcap?

a. a drink just before going to bed
b. something you wear for an evening walk
c. a flower
d. a black hat
e. midnight

16 Which word has a different sound?
a. boot
b. foot
c. shoot
d. root
e. flute

17 What is this dog wearing?
a. a hat
b. a coat
c. a collar
d. a scarf
e. a tie

18 Which of these is not a relation?
a. an aunt
b. an uncle
c. a friend
d. a brother
e. a sister

19 Which is wrong?
a. He likes often to go to a football match.
b. I meet him less often now.
c. We often go walking at weekends.
d. It seems to happen rather often.
e. Often I don't speak to them.

20 Which of these is made of paper?
a. a can
b. a paper clip
c. an envelope
d. a story
e. a pencil

Unit six

1 *England* is to *English* as *Germany* is to
a. German
b. Germany
c. Germanish
d. Dutch
e. Germish

2 The opposite of *come* is
a. came
b. went
c. leave
d. go
e. arrive

3 What has he done?
a. shot a fish
b. brought a fish
c. lifted a fish
d. found a fish
e. caught a fish

4 If you call a man Mick, his name is
a. Nicholas
b. Matthew
c. Mark
d. Michael
e. Richard

5 When you buy jam in Britain, it is usually in
a. a bottle
b. a glass
c. a bin
d. a jug
e. a jar

6 Which word does not go with the others?
a. wood
b. petrol
c. water
d. milk
e. beer

7 What is this?
a. a locker
b. a key
c. a lock
d. a handle
e. an opener

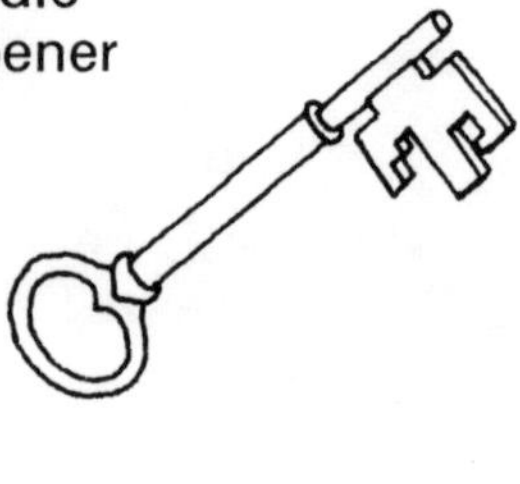

8 How many is a couple?
a. one
b. five
c. ten
d. twelve
e. two

9 Which word describes all the others?
a. tea
b. coffee
c. hot chocolate
d. cocoa
e. drink

10 Which is wrong?
a. I hope you have not forgotten.
b. Oh dear, I forgotted.
c. What has been forgotten?
d. I knew you would forget.
e. Yes, you did forget.

11 What is a ladybird?
a. a kind of lady
b. a kind of insect
c. a kind of bird
d. a kind of animal
e. a kind of fish

12 Which word does not go with all the others?
a. a noise
b. to hear
c. to see
d. ears
e. to listen

13 Which is wrong?
a. He fell unriderly.
b. The horse is riderless.
c. He was having a ride.
d. He was riding.
e. He's a poor rider.

14 The opposite of *cold* is
a. chilly
b. boiling
c. cool
d. hot
e. warm

15 Which word has the same sound as *cheat*?
a. ate
b. great
c. bleat
d. eight
e. plate

16 Which means the same as *to close*?
a. to fasten
b. to fill
c. to push
d. to shut
e. to open

17 Which is not true?
- a. She's going to run.
- b. She's looking ahead.
- c. Her feet are together.
- d. She's a runner.
- e. She's ready to run.

18 Which word has a different sound?
- a. fly
- b. eye
- c. buy
- d. weigh
- e. high

19 Which animal barks?
- a. a dog
- b. a cat
- c. a cow
- d. a mouse
- e. a pig

20 In which sentence does *get on* mean *succeed*?
- a. Time is getting on.
- b. He doesn't get on well with his wife.
- c. Get on your bicycle.
- d. Get on with your work.
- e. He's keen to get on at work.

Unit seven

1 Which word does not go with all the others?
a. birds
b. feathers
c. a nest
d. eggs
e. a house

2 Which is a boy's name?
a. Pauline
b. Mary
c. Margaret
d. Philip
e. Frances

3 Which is wrong?
a. She excites.
b. She's excited.
c. She's full of excitement.
d. She's jumping up and down excitedly.
e. She thinks it's exciting.

4 Which word has the same sound as *told*?
a. should
b. fooled
c. ruled
d. rolled
e. would

5 *Laugh* is to *cry* as *smile* is to
a. teeth
b. blink
c. whisper
d. stare
e. frown

6 Which word does not go with the others?
a. a flame
b. a blazer
c. a fire
d. to burn
e. hot

7 What is the answer when someone asks: *What dress did she wear?*
a. She have wore her purple dress.
b. She wore her purple dress.
c. She wored her purple dress.
d. She worn her purple dress.
e. She has worn her purple dress.

8 Which of these is part of your face?
a. your elbow
b. your knee
c. your wrist
d. your chin
e. your ankle

9 Which word has a different sound?

a. eight
b. light
c. might
d. fight
e. right

10 Which is right?

a. The wind is blowing.
b. The wind is pushing.
c. The wind is running.
d. The wind is going.
e. The wind is coming.

11 Which of these is yellow?

a. butter
b. ink
c. silver
d. an orange
e. milk

12 The opposite of *break* is

a. mend
b. broken
c. join
d. cure
e. fasten

13 What is she using?
a. a drawing pin
b. a nail
c. a point
d. a pin
e. a needle

14 Which word has a different sound?
a. done
b. none
c. one
d. gone
e. won

15 Which word describes all the others?
a. a vegetable
b. a potato
c. a carrot
d. a cabbage
e. a Brussels sprout

16 Which word does not go with all the others?
a. a bank
b. money
c. to save
d. a cheque
e. a river

17 What is he doing to the carpet?
a. shaking it
b. pulling it
c. pushing it
d. throwing it
e. showing it

☐

18 Which means the same as *to watch*?
a. to look for
b. to look at
c. to look out
d. to look in
e. to look down

☐

19 Choose the word which is found most often with *cup*.
a. handle
b. spoon
c. dish
d. plate
e. saucer

☐

20 Where does an actress work?
a. in a theatre
b. in an art gallery
c. in a factory
d. in a restaurant
e. in a town hall

☐

Unit eight

1 Where do you wear a scarf?
   a. round your waist
   b. round your wrist
   c. round your shoulders
   d. on your foot
   e. round your neck

2 When you are a customer, what are you doing?
   a. breaking something
   b. buying something
   c. making something
   d. eating something
   e. selling something

3 Which word does not go with all the others?
   a. a glove
   b. to wear
   c. an arm
   d. a hand
   e. warm

4 What are they doing?
   a. pressing hands
   b. shaking hands
   c. pulling hands
   d. shaking fingers
   e. holding hands

5 Which word has a different sound?

a. speak
b. weak
c. break
d. week
e. beak

6 Which of these is usually made of wool?

a. a sheep
b. a towel
c. a wardrobe
d. a kitten
e. a cardigan

7 The opposite of *early* is

a. soon
b. first
c. late
d. slow
e. last

8 What is he holding?

a. a record
b. a camera
c. a film
d. a recorder
e. a photographer

9 Which is wrong?
a. You shut the drawer.
b. You are shutting the drawer.
c. You have shut the drawer.
d. You shutted the drawer.
e. You did shut the drawer.

10 Which word does not go with all the others?
a. a comb
b. a stocking
c. hair
d. to tidy
e. to smooth

11 *Girl* is to *woman* as *girls* are to
a. womin
b. woman's
c. womans
d. women
e. woman

12 Where do you put a stamp?
a. on a newspaper
b. on a wall
c. on a shoe
d. on a book
e. on a letter

13 Which two words sound the same?
a. pail, pile
b. pall, pal
c. pall, pale
d. pail, pale
e. peal, pill

14 Who has something to do with a church?
a. a dancer
b. a model
c. a conductor
d. a vicar
e. a fireman

15 Where is he?
a. over the edge
b. on the edge
c. in the edge
d. near the edge
e. along the edge

16 Which of these is made of wood?
a. a mirror
b. a tin
c. a knife
d. a flower
e. a violin

17 *Forehead, chin* and *cheek* all have something to do with
a. the face
b. the body
c. ships
d. food
e. the mouth

18 What is this?
a. a beetle
b. a bee
c. a fly
d. an ant
e. a spider

19 Which word means the same as *easy*?
a. quick
b. comfortable
c. simple
d. difficult
e. hard

20 Which of these is smallest?
a. a pool
b. a puddle
c. a lake
d. the sea
e. a pond

Unit nine

1 Which word does not go with all the others?
a. a horse
b. a cow
c. a jockey
d. a race
e. to ride

2 Where is the flag?
a. at the top of the post
b. at the top of the pole
c. at the top of the mast
d. at the top of the stick
e. at the top of the rod

3 What is the opposite of *to lose*?
a. to forget
b. to remember
c. to find
d. to look for
e. to have

4 If you only go to the theatre occasionally, you go
a. now and again
b. again and again
c. once and again
d. time and again
e. then and again

5 Which two words sound the same?
a. plays, police
b. police, place
c. place, plaice
d. plays, place
e. police, plaice

6 Which word does not go with all the others?

a. a shoe
b. to clean
c. a sock
d. to brush
e. polish

☐

7 Which word does not go with all the others?

a. to watch
b. a television
c. a picture
d. to switch
e. a clock

☐

8 What is the answer when someone asks: *Did you understand it?*

a. Yes, I am understanding it.
b. Yes, I am understood it.
c. Yes, I have understanding it.
d. Yes, I understood it.
e. Yes, I have understand it.

☐

9 What is he doing?

a. hiding the money
b. missing the money
c. losing the money
d. putting the money
e. covering the money

☐

10 Which word means nearly the same as *little*?
a. thin
b. great
c. big
d. short
e. long

11 *Breakfast* is to *morning* as *lunch* is to
a. midday
b. night
c. morning
d. evening
e. afternoon

12 What is he using?
a. a duster
b. a broom
c. a brush
d. a rubber
e. a comb

13 Which of these is wrong?
a. the back of your hand
b. the back of a chair
c. the back of a penny
d. the back of a knife
e. the back of a book

14 What is the opposite of *over*?
a. above
b. below
c. beneath
d. less
e. under

15 Which of these is the shortest?

a. a minute
b. a week
c. an hour
d. a day
e. a second

16 Which word does not go with all the others?

a. a book
b. a library
c. to read
d. a title
e. to smell

17 What do you put on a pedal?

a. your nose
b. your leg
c. your hand
d. your head
e. your foot

18 Which word means the same as *afraid*?

a. fearful
b. fearless
c. to fear
d. fear
e. feared

19 Which word has a different sound?

a. wood
b. good
c. should
d. could
e. food

20 What are they doing?
a. pulling
b. hurting
c. pushing
d. fighting
e. hitting

Unit ten

1 Which of these is wrong?
a. a bunch of trees
b. a bunch of flowers
c. a bunch of bananas
d. a bunch of keys
e. a bunch of grapes

2 The opposite of *rough* is
a. hard
b. smooth
c. shiny
d. silky
e. sharp

3 What do we call the most important man on a ship?
a. the captain
b. the leader
c. the boss
d. the head
e. the governor

4 What is she doing?
a. working the car
b. making the car
c. driving the car
d. sending the car
e. operating the car

5 Where do you see a zebra crossing?
a. in the street
b. on the beach
c. in a zoo
d. in a field
e. in a museum

6 Which word does not go with all the others?
a. money
b. to spend
c. to buy
d. to pay
e. to shake

7 Which do we not use to make a cake?
a. sugar
b. flour
c. currants
d. soup
e. margarine

8 What is he doing?
a. washing down
b. washing out
c. washing over
d. washing up
e. washing

9 Which of these can you blow?
a. a horn
b. a violin
c. a guitar
d. a piano
e. a banjo

10 Which is wrong?
a. I don't anywhere want to meet her.
b. I cannot find my jacket anywhere,
c. Anywhere you go, you need money.
d. He cannot see a rose bush anywhere in the garden.
e. Put your bag down anywhere.

11 What colour is blood?
a. red
b. blue
c. orange
d. yellow
e. green

12 What do you put on a pillow?
a. your hand
b. your leg
c. your foot
d. your head
e. your back

13 Which is wrong?
a. The postman carried a letter.
b. The postman losed a letter.
c. The postman delivered a letter.
d. The postman left a letter.
e. The postman brought a letter.

14 Four of these are common British trees: which is not?
a. palm
b. ash
c. beech
d. elm
e. oak

15 What is she?
a. a waitress
b. a cleaner
c. a secretary
d. a headmistress
e. a nurse

16 Which word has the same sound as *height*?

a. eight
b. hate
c. feat
d. sleet
e. white

17 Where is the picture?

a. on the wall
b. in the wall
c. near the wall
d. at the wall
e. by the wall

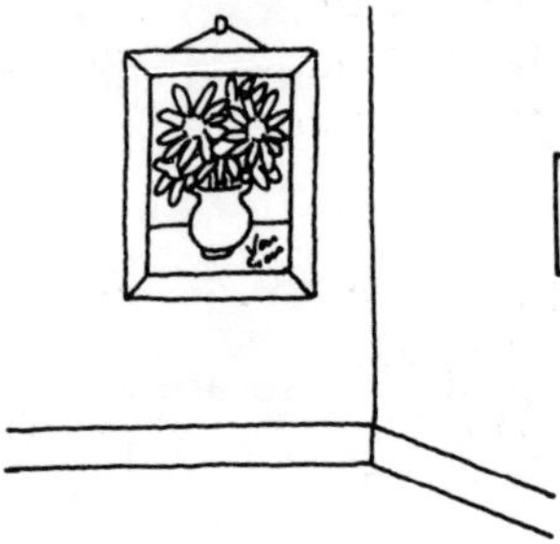

18 Which of these can you read?

a. a bookshelf
b. a library
c. a film
d. a picture
e. a dictionary

19 When you find something, you

a. cover it
b. re-cover it
c. recover it
d. uncover it
e. discover it

20 Which word means *by yourself*?

a. just
b. almost
c. alone
d. along
e. lonely

Unit eleven

1 What does a dentist do to a bad tooth?
a. take it off
b. take it out
c. take it away
d. take it in
e. take it over

2 Which is a boy's name?
a. Susan
b. Elaine
c. Caroline
d. Christopher
e. Jean

3 Which of these is cold?
a. steam
b. leather
c. rubber
d. ice
e. water

4 What is she doing?
a. working the tap
b. turning the tap on
c. making the tap
d. doing the tap
e. operating the tap

5 Which of these does not go with all the others?
a. a light
b. a book
c. to switch on
d. a shadow
e. electricity

6 A room inside the roof of a house is called
a. a basement
b. a cellar
c. a hall
d. an attic
e. a workshop

7 The opposite of *broad* is
a. wide
b. slim
c. fat
d. narrow
e. thin

8 What is she saying?
a. Take it off me!
b. Take me it off!
c. Take it me off!
d. Take me off it!
e. Take off me it!

9 Which word has a different sound?
a. stone
b. phone
c. shone
d. bone
e. alone

10 One *child*, but two
a. child
b. childer
c. childs'
d. child's
e. children

11 Which word describes all the others?
a. a sandal
b. a boot
c. footwear
d. a slipper
e. a plimsoll

12 Which is not true?
a. She isn't running.
b. She's carrying a coat.
c. Her basket is on the ground.
d. Her basket is on her left.
e. She's a fat lady.

13 Which is wrong?
a. I am holding the case.
b. I cannot hold the case.
c. I had hold the case.
d. I held the case.
e. I hold the case.

14 Which word does not go with all the others?
a. a sigh
b. to play
c. sad
d. to breathe
e. a sound

15 Which word has the same sound as *though*?
a. cough
b. show
c. trough
d. through
e. do

16 Which means the same as *to approach*?
a. to go towards
b. to go in
c. to go out
d. to go round
e. to go down

17 The opposite of *back* is
a. forward
b. come
c. behind
d. front
e. side

18 What is this?

a. a cigarette holder
b. a cigarette tray
c. an ash-pan
d. an ashtray
e. a cigarette case

19 Which is wrong?

a. They are never at home on Sundays.
b. I have never seen so many people here before.
c. We can hear our neighbour's radio but it is never loud.
d. Never mind about him.
e. She always invites me, but never I go.

20 *Seaside, swimsuit* and *paddle* all have something to do with

a. winter
b. the countryside
c. a job
d. a hobby
e. holidays

Unit twelve

1 Which is not part of a car?
a. a wheel
b. a tyre
c. a driver
d. headlamps
e. a boot

2 Which two words sound the same?
a. pane, pain
b. pain, pine
c. pine, pin
d. pan, pane
e. pen, pain

3 Which of these does not have legs?
a. a bee
b. a horse
c. a table
d. a pair of trousers
e. an aeroplane

4 What is she doing?
a. brushing her teeth
b. the brushing
c. teeth-brushing
d. brushing teeth
e. brushing the teeth

5 Which meal can be eaten at any time of day?
a. breakfast
b. lunch
c. dinner
d. tea
e. a snack

6 What is the opposite of *heavy*?
a. light
b. comfortable
c. smooth
d. easy
e. soft

7 Which is right?
a. The sun is looking.
b. The sun is showing.
c. The sun is shining.
d. The sun is outing.
e. The sun is watching.

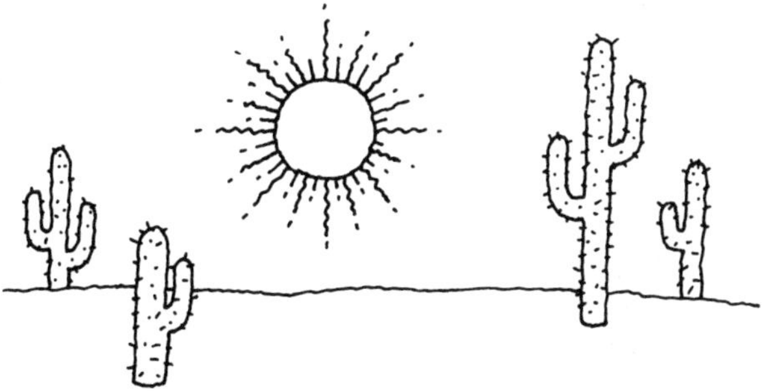

8 Which word means something like *a mountain*?
a. a hill
b. a rock
c. a river
d. a top
e. a valley

9 Which is a girl's name?
a. David
b. Alan
c. Philip
d. Francis
e. Judith

10 Which is wrong?
a. Even if you pay me I will not come.
b. I don't even enjoy beer now.
c. I never even saw him leave.
d. Please even don't mention it.
e. Even her friends cannot help her.

11 Which word does not go with all the others?
a. a film
b. to shut
c. a camera
d. a photograph
e. an album

12 Which of these is not a colour?
a. dark
b. green
c. grey
d. blue
e. red

13 What is she doing?
a. delivering a letter
b. sending a letter
c. reading a letter
d. posting a letter
e. writing a letter

14 Which is wrong?
  a. I have a sore throat.
  b. I have a headache.
  c. I have a surprise for you.
  d. I have hunger.
  e. I have a gun.

15 Where does a cook work?
  a. in a garage
  b. in a church
  c. in a kitchen
  d. in a market
  e. in a shop

16 Which word has a different sound?
  a. please
  b. knees
  c. police
  d. cheese
  e. keys

17 What is the opposite of *to teach*?
  a. to show
  b. to know
  c. to listen
  d. to learn
  e. to understand

18 What is she saying?
  a. Get off!
  b. Getting up!
  c. Get down!
  d. Get up!
  e. Get in!

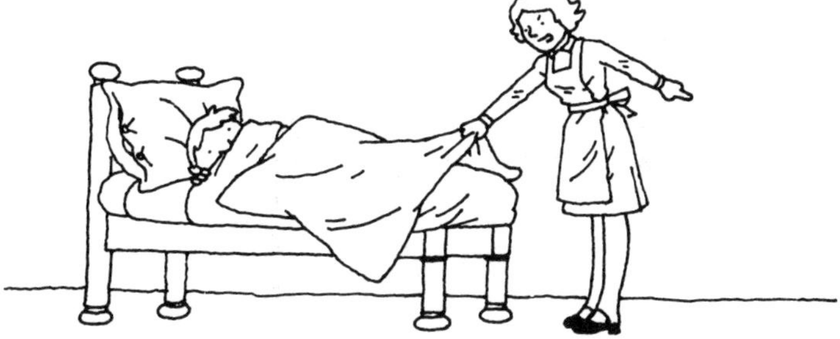

19 The American word *vacation* means the same as the English word

a. holiday
b. call
c. vacant
d. weekend
e. empty

20 Which do we not say?

a. I like football.
b. I like cricket.
c. I like tennis.
d. I like rugby.
e. I like swim.

Unit thirteen

1 Which is not true?

a. The shelf is too high.
b. He is too short.
c. He can't reach the bottles.
d. Neither bottle is full.
e. He is climbing the wall.

2 Which is not part of your face?
a. your eye
b. your nose
c. your mouth
d. your neck
e. your chin

3 Which of these means nearly the same as *a pool*?
a. to swim
b. water
c. wet
d. a lake
e. rain

4 Which of these has no wings?
a. a mosquito
b. a fly
c. a bee
d. a butterfly
e. a worm

5 When you give a right answer, you are
a. honest
b. just
c. correct
d. true
e. well

6 Which word does not go with all the others?
a. snow
b. white
c. soon
d. cold
e. to fall

7 The opposite of *mean* is
a. generous
b. thin
c. foolish
d. cruel
e. weak

8 What is he using?
a. a knife
b. a saw
c. scissors
d. a blade
e. an axe

9 Which is wrong?
a. She ran fastly.
b. She got up slowly.
c. She spoke quietly.
d. She cried miserably.
e. She climbed carefully.

10 Which two words sound the same?
a. grade, greet
b. grade, great
c. great, greet
d. great, grate
e. grade, grate

11 Which is wrong?
   a. He meets people every day.
   b. I am meetting you tomorrow.
   c. I met him yesterday.
   d. He has met my friend.
   e. Meet me at three o'clock.

12 What is this?
   a. a there and back ticket
   b. a double ticket
   c. a return ticket
   d. a twin ticket
   e. a returning ticket

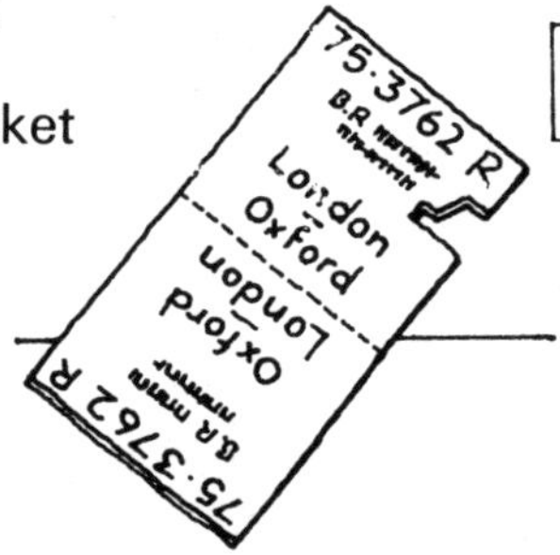

13 Instead of *gradually* or *slowly*, we can say
   a. little by little
   b. little and little
   c. little after little
   d. little plus little
   e. little to little

14 The opposite of *young* is
   a. weak
   b. long
   c. big
   d. old
   e. new

15 Which word does not go with all the others?
a. cheese
b. butter
c. coffee
d. milk
e. cream

16 Which is a girl's name?
a. Peter
b. Anthony
c. Gillian
d. Mark
e. Paul

17 Which word has a different sound?
a. clear
b. dear
c. wear
d. near
e. hear

18 What is she saying?
a. You are like it, aren't you?
b. You are like it, don't you?
c. You like it, liken't you?
d. You like it, isn't it?
e. You like it, don't you?

19 Boxers fight in a boxing
a. ring
b. circle
c. square
d. box
e. cycle

20 Which do we not say?
a. I can feel something hard.
b. I feel chilly.
c. I feel to go dancing.
d. I feel sorry for him.
e. I can feel rain.

Unit fourteen

1 Which do you never see at an airport?
a. a steward
b. a passport
c. a lighthouse
d. a pilot
e. a ticket

2 This glass is
a. empty
b. open
c. water
d. full
e. filled

3 Which word does not go with all the others?
a. to cry
b. a needle
c. cotton
d. to mend
e. to tear

4 *Saddle, rider* and *hoof* all have something to do with
a. elephants
b. horses
c. walking
d. sheep
e. bicycles

5 Which word has a different sound?
a. flour
b. door
c. four
d. floor
e. more

6 Which does not have a lid?
a. a cupboard
b. a box
c. a tin
d. an eye
e. a dustbin

7 Which is not true?
a. He's swimming.
b. He's having a swim.
c. He's having a bath.
d. He's bathing.
e. He's having a bathe.

8 Which of these is not part of the day?
a. morning
b. afternoon
c. today
d. evening
e. night

9 Two runners finishing a race together are
a. neck alongside neck
b. neck against neck
c. neck by neck
d. neck and neck
e. neck to neck

10 The opposite of *clean* is
a. filthy
b. wet
c. muddy
d. dirty
e. damp

11 Which is wrong?
a. He's going asleep.
b. He's falling asleep.
c. He's asleep.
d. He's sleeping.
e. He's going to sleep.

12 Which two words sound the same?
a. male, mile
b. mile, meal
c. mile, mail
d. mail, male
e. meal, male

13 Which word does not go with all the others?

a. a gun
b. sad
c. to shoot
d. to kill
e. a bullet

14 What is he doing?

a. painting
b. cleaning
c. drinking
d. drawing
e. brushing

15 Which is wrong?

a. I am always breaking cups and saucers.
b. I will remember you always.
c. It always happens at this time of year.
d. Although he has troubles he is always pleasant.
e. Always Christmas is in December.

16 What is the answer when someone asks: *Were you there last week?*

a. Yes, I am.
b. Yes, I was.
c. Yes, I be.
d. Yes, I been.
e. Yes, I being.

17 These people are waiting at
a. a bus stand
b. a bus halt
c. a bus place
d. a bus stop
e. a bus station

18 Starting with the weakest, the correct order for these drinks is
a. lemonade, beer, wine, whisky
b. lemonade, whisky, beer, wine
c. beer, wine, lemonade, whisky
d. wine, lemonade, whisky, beer
e. lemonade, wine, beer, whisky

19 Which word means the same as *hard*?
a. differently
b. difference
c. difficult
d. difficulty
e. different

20 *A lounge* is another name for
a. a dining room
b. a bedroom
c. a kitchen
d. a study
e. a sitting room

Unit fifteen

1 Which of these can you throw?
a. a ball
b. rain
c. air
d. a house
e. a car

2 Which word is nearest in meaning to *narrow*?
a. short
b. thin
c. broad
d. wide
e. fat

3 What is this?
a. a hen
b. a duck
c. a chicken
d. a goose
e. a swan

4 Which word has a different sound?
a. fair
b. fare
c. hair
d. hare
e. fur

5 Which is wrong?
   a. I flied there.
   b. I travelled there.
   c. I rode there.
   d. I drove there.
   e. I hurried there.

6 Which of these does not grow on a tree?
   a. a pear
   b. a peach
   c. a plum
   d. an apricot
   e. a redcurrant

7 Which is not true?
   a. He is looking at the ground.
   b. He isn't looking where he is going.
   c. There's going to be an accident.
   d. He hasn't seen the notice.
   e. He should be more careful.

8 Which is a boy's name?
a. Janet
b. James
c. Jean
d. Jane
e. Joan

☐

9 Which of these sells meat?
a. a greengrocer
b. a florist
c. a baker
d. a butcher
e. a grocer

☐

10 What do you do with a shoelace?
a. eat it
b. open it
c. tie it
d. wear it
e. polish it

☐

11 Which word does not go with all the others?
a. a football
b. a goal
c. a player
d. a light
e. a match

☐

12 What is the opposite of *high*?
a. over
b. under
c. low
d. up
e. down

☐

13 Which is not true?
a. His elbows are on the desk.
b. He's sitting at a desk.

c. The drawers are shut.
d. The lamp is on his right.
e. There are six drawers

14 Which of these is wet?

a. chalk
b. dust
c. powder
d. a puddle
e. a biscuit

15 Which two words sound the same?

a. pause, pose
b. poise, pies
c. pose, poise
d. paws, pose
e. paws, pause

16 When you put the knives, forks and spoons on the table, what are you doing?

a. placing the table
b. laying the table
c. making the table
d. doing the table
e. putting the table

17 What is the opposite of *to start*?
a. to begin
b. to die
c. to halt
d. to commence
e. to stop

18 Which is correct?
a. He is wearing spectacles.
b. He is wearing the spectacles.
c. He is wearing a spectacles.
d. He wears spectacles.
e. He wears a spectacles.

19 We say one *foot*, but two
a. feet
b. feet's
c. feets
d. foot
e. feets'

20 *House* is to *chimney* as *ship* is to
a. funnel
b. smoker
c. steamer
d. chimney
e. sail

Answer section

Lautschriftzeichen

[ˈ]	steht vor der betonten Silbe
[ː]	bezeichnet einen langen Vokal
[i]	wie in **big** [big]
[iː]	wie in **see** [siː]
[e]	wie in **pen** [pen]
[æ]	wie in **man** [mæn]
[ɑː]	wie in **arm** [ɑːm]
[ɔ]	wie in **not** [nɔt]
[ɔː]	wie in **walk** [wɔːk]
[u]	wie in **book** [buk]
[uː]	wie in **two** [tuː]
[ʌ]	wie in **cut** [kʌt]
[əː]	wie in **word** [wəːd]
[ə]	wie in **about** [əˈbaut]
[ei]	wie in **day** [dei]
[əu]	wie in **go** [gəu]
[ai]	wie in **my** [mai]
[au]	wie in **how** [hau]
[ɔi]	wie in **boy** [bɔi]
[iə]	wie in **here** [hiə]
[ɛə]	wie in **wear** [wɛə]
[uə]	wie in **sure** [ʃuə]

[p] wie in **pen** [pen]
[b] wie in **big** [big]
[t] wie in **ten** [ten]
[d] wie in **dog** [dɔg]
[k] wie in **cat** [kæt]
[g] wie in **go** [gəu]
[tʃ] wie in **church** [tʃə:tʃ]
[dʒ] wie in **John** [dʒɔn]
[f] wie in **fan** [fæn]
[v] wie in **van** [væn]
[θ] wie in **thin** [θin]
[ð] wie in **then** [ðen]
[s] wie in **sit** [sit]
[z] wie in **zoo** [zu:]
[ʃ] wie in **shoe** [ʃu:]
[ʒ] wie in **measure** [ˈmeʒə]
[h] wie in **hot** [hɔt]
[m] wie in **my** [mai]
[n] wie in **no** [nəu]
[ŋ] wie in **long** [lɔŋ]
[l] wie in **leg** [leg]
[r] wie in **run** [rʌn]
[j] wie in **you** [ju:]
[w] wie in **when** [wen]

Answers

Unit one

1 **c.** *Shortly* and *soon* = in a little while. *At present* = now. *Later* = not immediately.
2 **d.** *Cotton* is used with a needle for sewing. *String* is used for fastening parcels. *Rope* is much stronger and is used on ships.
3 **c.** *Catched* is wrong.
4 **b.** The eye may be *green* or *yellow, blue* or *purple*. But we always say *a black eye*.
5 **b.** The opposite of *many* = *few*. The opposite of *a little* = *a lot*.
6 **a**
7 **d.** We *eat* when we are *hungry*. We *drink* when we are *thirsty*.
8 **c.** The *door* is part of the house. The *plane, sky* and *sun* are above the house.
9 **e.** We can *catch fish* with *a net*. Fish live in the *sea*.
10 **c.** *A knob* = a round handle.

a doorknob

11 **d.** You can drink *petrol* and *ink*, but they are dangerous. *Paper* and *ice* are not liquid: it is impossible to drink them.

12 **a.** *Sleepable* is not an English word. All the others are correct.

13 **d.** The other four describe the weather.

14 **a.** *Well* [wel] and *will* [wil] have short sounds. *Wheel* and *we'll* have a long sound [wiːl].

15 **c.** The opposite of *asleep* = awake. The opposite of *ill* = well. *Blind* = not able to see. The opposite of *quiet* = noisy.

16 **b.** *A carrier* is usually made of strong paper, and has handles. *A basket* is made of cane and often has a handle. *A bin* is usually made of metal, often without a handle. *A holder* is usually a small thing (a cigarette holder, a pen holder).

17 **a.** *A train* carries *passengers* from one *station* to another. Trains run on *rails*.

18 **b.** We *ask* for something when we *want* it. When we *like* something, we think it is pleasant. *Wanting* something is much stronger: the thing seems to be necessary (to want a new coat, to need a new coat). *To fail* = the opposite of to succeed.

19 **c.** *Work* [wəːk] has a different sound. All the others have the same sound in the middle and at the end.

20 **b.** *Take your hand off* = Take your hand away. *They took 10% off the bill* = They made the bill 10% smaller. *He never took his eyes off her* = He never stopped looking at her. *She took off her shoes* = She took her shoes off her feet.

Unit two

1 **a.** *A mechanic* works with cars and machines (a car mechanic works in a garage). *A workman* = any man who works with his hands. *An assistant* = a man or woman who helps someone (a shop assistant who helps customers; a dentist's assistant).

2 **e.** *Flowers* and *grass grow* in *gardens.*
3 **b.** *Winking* is always deliberate, never an accident. You sometimes wink at someone because you like them, or to be friendly.
4 **d.** *Towards* = in the direction of (to walk towards the door). *Above* = over (a plane above the clouds). *Between* = in the middle (two is between one and three). *Beside* = at the side of (to sit beside someone).
5 **c.** If you call a man *Jack*, his name is *John*. If you call him Harry, his name is *Harold*. If you call him Gerry, his name is *Gerald*.
6 **d.** We *put off* (or turn off) *a light*. We put out *fires, matches, candles* and *cigarette lighters*.
7 **d.** We drink all the others.

8 **c.** When we eat food, it goes into the *stomach*.

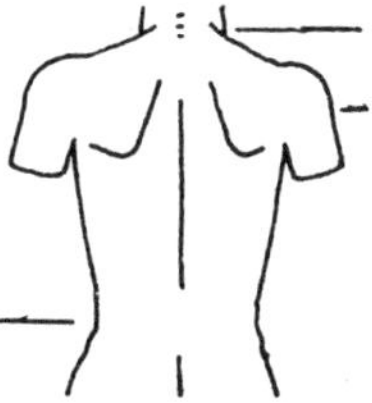

9 **c.** The opposite of *low* = high. *Silent* = quiet. The opposite of *calm* = rough. The opposite of *noisy* = quiet.
10 **d.** *A counter* = the long table between the assistant and the customer.
11 **a.** *Height* [hait] has a different sound. The other words have the same sound as *weight* [weit].
12 **c.** We use a dustpan and brush together.

All these are for cleaning. *A duster* = a dry cloth. *A dishcloth* = a cloth for washing dishes.

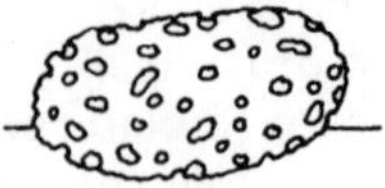

a sponge

a mop

13 **d.** When you *hold* a ladder, one end may be on the ground. When you *hold it up*, you lift it up high. When you *lift it*, you pick it up. When you *walk under it*, the top of the ladder is against a wall and you do not touch it. (People sometimes say this brings bad luck.)

14 **c.** *Glad* = happy. The opposite of *hard* = soft. The opposite of *heavy* = light (weight). The opposite of *dark* = light (colour).

15 **a.** *A timetable* gives the times of trains, planes, lessons, etc. *A dressing table* is used in a bedroom.

16 **e**

a rabbit

17 **d.** *I am going to make my hair* is wrong. We do our hair, comb it or brush it. *Make up your mind!* = Decide!

18 **c.** *A cleaner* = a person who cleans; also, a machine that cleans (a vacuum cleaner). The others have no meaning.

19 **a.** *Sure* = certain. *Untrue* = false; also, not faithful.

20 **c.** Notice: *few* [fjuː], *long* [lɔŋ], *vague* [veig], *orange* [ˈɔrindʒ]; but *tongue* [tʌŋ] and *hung* [hʌŋ].

Unit three

1 **d.** *A spinster* = an unmarried woman. *A niece* = your brother's or sister's daughter. *An actress* = a woman actor. *A nun* = a woman who belongs to a group of women working for God.

2 **c.** The opposite of *beginning* = *end*. The opposite of *start* = *finish*.

3 **b.** *An audience* = many people, never one, listening together, usually in a theatre or cinema. A lot of people *in church* = a congregation. People *at a football match* = spectators.

4 **e.** *Shoe* [ʃuː] has the same sound as *through* [θruː]. *Rough* [rʌf], *enough* [iˈnʌf] and *tough* [tʌf] have the same sound.

5 **e.** *On the table* = on top of it. *Under the table* = with the table on top of them. The others are impossible.

6 **e.** We wear *shoes* on our *feet*. Shoes often have *laces*, which we *tie*. A man often wears *a tie* round his neck.

7 **a.** *A smoother* is not an English word. *A presser* = someone who presses clothes. *A clothes press* = a large machine for pressing clothes. *A press* = a machine for pressing (a wine press); also, a machine for printing books and newspapers.

8 **b.** *Plums* are dark red or yellow and grow on trees. *Cabbages* and *cauliflowers* grow above the ground. *Carrots* and *beetroots* grow in the ground.

9 **a.** *A month* = a twelfth part of a year (January is the first month). There are four seasons in the year.
10 **b.** *The car picked up speed* = The car went faster. *She picked herself up* = She stood up again. *I'll pick you up* = I'll come for you. *He picked up his hat* = He took it in his hand.
11 **c.** The correct sentence is: *I showed you the way.*
12 **e.** *Straight* [streit] has a different sound. The others all have the same sound as *white* [wait].
13 **a.** *Pick up it!* is not good English.
14 **d.** We *sleep* in *bed* at *night* and sometimes *dream.*
15 **b.** *Stairs* = a number of fixed steps, usually inside a building. *Steps* are usually outside, but often there is one step at the entrance to a building.
16 **e.** All these are animals, but only *a tiger* is dangerous.
17 **c.** Notice: *now and again* and *now and then* = *sometimes*, occasionally. *Soon* = in a short time.
18 **c.** We *collect* or *gather* flowers, sea-shells and pieces of wood (we walk about looking for them), but we collect (do not gather) stamps, postcards, etc. A crowd collected, or, a crowd gathered = many people came together. *To connect* = to join (to connect two wires).
19 **e.** *Bald* = without hair (a bald man, a bald head). *Don't lose your temper!* = Don't get angry; Keep cool!
20 **e.** The *untrue* thing is *unbelievable*, not *believable.*

Unit four

1 **b.** *Apples, oranges, lemons* and *pears* are all fruits that grow on trees.

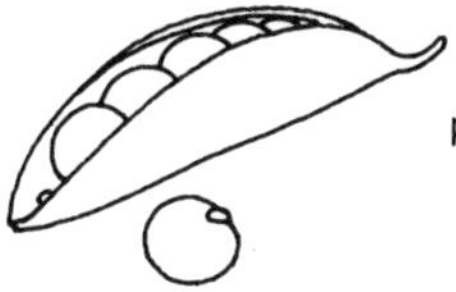

peas

2 **b.** People never say this. All the others are correct and mean the same thing.

3 **a.** The opposite of *to give* = *to take*. The opposite of *to lend* = to borrow.

4 **a.** *Bowl* [bəul] and *roll* [rəul] have the same sound. *Howl* [haul] and *owl* [aul] have the same sound. But *rule* [ruːl] and *fall* [fɔːl] are different.

5 **d.** *A van* = a closed lorry for carrying things by road (a furniture van). All the others have two wheels.

6 **a.** *Helicopters* and *planes fly*; *a fly* can fly but it is an insect and has no *engine*.

a fly

7 **b.** Telephones and bells *ring*. Whistles and trumpets *sound*. Only people *call, sing* and *speak*.

8 **e.** *Dogs wag* their *tails* when they are *happy*. *Cats* wag their tails when they are angry.

9 **e.** We ride in or on *boats* and *trains*. We ride in *a car*. We cannot ride *wolves*.

10 **a.** This is incorrect. The correct sentence is: *I have lent her money.*
11 **d.** *Where* [wɛə] is different. *Were* [wəː], *her* [həː], *sir* [səː] and *fur* [fəː] have the same sound.
12 **a.** The correct phrase here is: *as usual.*
13 **b.** You climb a rope *hand over hand*. The other phrases are not used.
14 **d.** The others are not correct.
15 **b**
16 **b.** *A pile* = an untidy collection of things, on top of each other.
17 **a**
18 **e.** The others are all *clothes*.
19 **e.** *A bar of soap* and *a cake of soap* = a piece of soap. But *a bar* and *a cake* alone never mean soap. *A towel* = a cloth for drying the hands after washing. *A washer* = a machine for washing clothes or dishes.
20 **a.** Notice: big, bigger, biggest; *good, better, best*; *bad, worse, worst*. So the opposite of best = worst.

Unit five

1 **a.** *A tumbler* = a flat-bottomed drinking glass (a tumbler of water).
2 **d.** We *sneeze* into *a handkerchief* when we have *a cold* in the *nose*. The opposite of *hot* = cold (hot weather, cold weather). But *hot* does not go with the other words.
3 **b.** All the others are wrong.
4 **a.** We never say *a clean day* (we can say: dirty weather, or, a dirty day).
5 **e.** The opposite of *easy* = difficult. The opposite of *pleasant* = unpleasant. The opposite of *beautiful* = ugly. The opposite of *comfortable* = uncomfortable.

6 a. We *wrap a parcel* with *paper* and *string*. Notice: we never wrap *a letter*.

7 **e.** *Also* and *too* = as well. *A toe* = part of the foot. *Two* = 2.

8 **e.** All these are meat. *Beef* is from a cow. *Lamb* is from a young sheep, a lamb. *Mutton* is from a sheep. *Veal* is from a young cow, a calf.

9 **c.** All the others are correct and mean the same thing.

10 **a.** The correct answers are: *I brought it*, or, *I have brought it*.

11 **b.** The correct sentence is: *He talked loudly. Aloudly* is not an English word. Aloud = not silently. Loudly = *noisily*.

12 **c.** *A chapter* = part of a book. *A paragraph* = part of a chapter. *A sentence* = part of a paragraph. *A word* = part of a sentence. *A letter* = part of a word.

13 **a.** *At the corner* and *on the corner* = outside the two walls (at or on the corner of the street). *By the corner* and *near the corner* = not far from the corner (the shop by the corner).

14 **d.** *A railway porter* carries passengers' luggage to and from trains.

15 **a**

16 **b.** *Foot* [fut] has a different sound. The others all have a long sound [buːt, ʃuːt, ruːt, fluːt].

17 **c.** Dogs often wear leather *collars* round their necks.

18 **c.** The others are all in the family. *Uncles* and *aunts* = your parents' *brothers* and *sisters*.

19 **a.** The correct sentence is: *He often likes to go to a football match.*

20 **c.** *A can* is made of metal. *A paper clip* is made of wire. *A story* is made of words. *A pencil* is made of wood and graphite.

Unit six

1 **a.** *Dutch* is the language of Holland. *Germany* is a country. *Germanish* and *Germish* are not English words.
2 **d.** The opposite of *came* = *went*. The opposite of *to leave* = *to arrive*.
3 **e.** Fishermen *catch* fish. We *shoot* things with a gun.
4 **d.** *Mick* is the short name for *Michael*. The other short names are Nick (*Nicholas*), Matt (*Matthew*), and Dick or Rick (*Richard*).
5 **e**

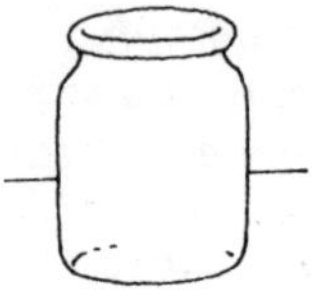
a jar

a bottle

a glass

a bin

a jug

6 **a.** *Wood* is a solid. All the others are liquid.
7 **b.** *A key* fits in *a lock*. *A locker* = a small cupboard with a lock. *An opener* = a metal tool to open things (a bottle opener, a can opener).
8 **e.** *Twelve* = a dozen.
9 **e**
10 **b.** The correct sentence is: *Oh dear, I forgot.*
11 **b**

a ladybird

12 **c.** We *listen to* and *hear noise* with our *ears*. We *see* with our eyes.

13 **a.** *Ride, rider, riding* and *riderless* are all correct. *Unriderly* is not an English word.

14 **d.** All these words are used about the weather. *Chilly* = cold. *Boiling* = very hot. *Cool* = rather cold. *Warm* = rather hot.

15 **c.** *Bleat* [bli:t] and *cheat* [tʃi:t] have the same sound. The others have the same sound [greit, eit, pleit] except for *ate* [et].

16 **d**

17 **c.** All the others describe the picture.

18 **d.** *Weigh* [wei] has a different sound. The others all have the same sound [flai, ai, bai, hai].

19 **a.** *A cat* miaows. *A cow* moos. *A mouse* squeaks. *A pig* grunts.

20 **e.** *Time is getting on* = Time is passing quickly. *He doesn't get on well with his wife* = He doesn't have a happy life with his wife. *Get on your bicycle* = Sit on your bicycle and ride it. *Get on with your work* = Continue with your work.

Unit seven

1 **e.** *Birds* have *feathers* and lay their *eggs* in *nests*.

2 **d.** All the others are girls' names. Notice: *Frances* for a girl, Francis for a boy.

3 **a.** The correct sentence is: *She is excited.*

4 **d.** *Rolled* [rəuld] and *told* [təuld] have the same sound. *Should* [ʃud] and *would* [wud] have the same sound. *Fooled* [fu:ld] and *ruled* [ru:ld] have the same sound.

5 **e.** The opposite of *to laugh* = *to cry*. The opposite of *to smile* = *to frown. To blink* = to shut the eyes quickly and for a very short time.

To whisper = to talk very quietly. *To stare* = to look long and hard.

6 **b.** *A blazer* = a light jacket, often with silver buttons.

7 **b.** *She has worn her purple dress* is also a correct sentence, but it is not the correct answer here. A question like *Which dress did she wear?*, must have an answer beginning *She wore*.

8 **d.** The *chin* = the part of the face under the mouth. The others are all joints. The *elbow* is in the middle of the arm. The *wrist* joins the hand to the arm. The *knee* is in the middle of the leg. The *ankle* joins the foot to the leg.

9 **a.** *Eight* [eit] has a different sound from *light* [lait], *might* [mait], *fight* [fait] and *right* [rait].

10 **a.** When there is a wind, this is the only correct sentence. *The wind is coming* = the wind is going to blow.

11 **a.** *Ink* is blue, black or red, etc. *Silver* is silver. *An orange* is orange. *Milk* is white.

12 **a.** The opposite of *broken* = mended. The oppósite of *fasten* = unfasten. *Join* and *cure* have no clear opposites.

13 **e.** The sharp end of *pins* and *nails* is the *point*.

a drawing pin a nail a pin

14 **d.** *Gone* [gɔn] is different. *Done* [dʌn], *none* [nʌn], *one* [wʌn] and *won* [wʌn] all have the same sound.

15 **a.** *Potatoes* and *carrots* = vegetables that grow in the ground. *Cabbages* and *sprouts* = green vegetables.

16 **e.** We *save money* in the *bank* and pay money out by *cheque*. (Also, a bank = the side of *a river*.)
17 **a**
18 **b.** *To look for* = to try to find. *To look out* = to be careful.
19 **e.** *Cup* and *saucer* are used together and so we often say them together.
20 **a.** *An actress* = a lady actor.

Unit eight

1 **e**
2 **b**
3 **c.** We *wear gloves* on our *hands* to keep them *warm*.
4 **b.** *Pressing hands* and *pulling hands* have no meaning. You *shake a finger* at someone when you are angry with him or want to control him. Lovers *hold hands*.
5 **c.** *Break* [breik] has a different sound. *Speak* [spiːk], *weak* [wiːk], *week* [wiːk] and *beak* [biːk] have the same sound.
6 **e.** *A cardigan* = a woollen jacket with buttons down the front. *A sheep* is covered with wool. *A towel* is made of cotton. *A wardrobe* = a clothes cupboard, made of wood. *A kitten* = a young cat.
7 **c.** The opposite of *first* = *last*. The opposite of *slow* = fast.
8 **b.** *A record* = a disc for playing on a gramophone or record player. *A film* = the special paper we put in *cameras* to take photographs. *A recorder* = a wooden musical instrument, like a flute; also, a tape recorder. *A photographer* = a person who takes photographs.
9 **d.** The correct sentence is: *You shut the drawer.*

10 **b.** We make our *hair smooth* and *tidy* with *a comb*. We wear *stockings* on our legs.
11 **d.** One *woman*, but two *women*. *Woman's* = of the woman (the woman's husband).
12 **e.** *Stamps* = the small paper squares we stick on the envelope to send a letter. Notice: to stamp = to hit the ground hard with the foot.
13 **d.** *Pail* [peil] and *pale* [peil] sound the same. *Pile* [pail], *pall* [pɔːl], *pal* [pæl], *peal* [piːl], and *pill* [pil] are different.
14 **d.** *A vicar* = a Church of England priest.
15 **b.** *Over the edge* = off the edge. *In the edge* is not possible. *Near the edge* = close to the edge. *Along the edge* = at the edge for a distance (to walk along the edge).
16 **e.** *A mirror* is made of glass. *A tin* and *a knife* are made of metal.
17 **a**

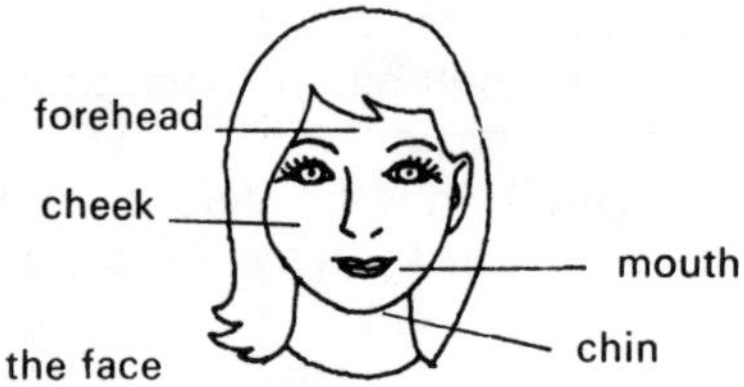

18 **b**
19 **c.** *Quick* = fast. *Comfortable* = physically at ease. *Difficult* and *hard* = not easy.
20 **b.** *A puddle* = a little water on the ground (rain leaves puddles). *A pool* = a small round patch of liquid usually spilt accidentally (a pool of milk, of oil, of blood); also, a small man-made lake (a swimming pool, a boating pool). *A lake* = a large natural stretch of water (Lake Superior is in North America). *The sea* = a very large stretch of salt water (the Mediterranean Sea, the Black Sea). *A pond* = a small stretch of water (a fish-pond, a duck-pond).

Unit nine

1 **b.** *A jockey rides a horse* in *a race.*

2 **c.** *A mast* = a long wooden pole on a ship which carries the sails. *A post* = a shorter, thicker piece of wood fixed in the ground (a gate post). *A pole* = a longer piece of wood, sometimes fixed in the ground (a telegraph pole, a flag pole). *A stick* = any short, thin piece of wood (a walking stick, a match stick). *A rod* = a long, thin piece of wood or metal (a fishing rod, a steel rod).

3 **c.** The opposite of *to forget* = *to remember. To look for* = to try *to find.*

4 **a.** *Again and again* and *time and again* = very often. The others are not good English.

5 **c.** *Place* [pleis] and *plaice* [pleis] sound the same. *Plays* [pleiz] and *police* [pəˈliːs] are different.

6 **c.** We *clean shoes* with *polish* and *a brush.*

7 **e.** We *switch* the *television* on *to watch* the *pictures.*

8 **d.** The others are not good English.

9 **a.** *To hide* = to put in a secret place.

10 **d.** The opposite of *short* = *long,* or tall. So, a *little* man = a short man. The opposite of *thin* = fat. *Great* = *big,* important.

11 **a.** We eat *breakfast* in the *morning.* We eat *lunch* at *midday.*

12 **c.** *A duster* = a dry cloth. *A broom* = a long-handled brush for sweeping floors. *A rubber* = a small piece of rubber for removing pencil marks. We make our hair tidy with *a comb.*

13 **c.** *A penny* (or any coin) does not have a front and *a back.* It has two sides: heads and tails. *Hands, chairs, knives* and *books* all have backs.

14 **e.** The opposite of *above* = *below. Beneath* = *under,* lower than. The opposite of *less*

= more. Notice: sometimes *less than* is the opposite of *over* (over ten pounds, less than ten pounds).

15 **e.** Sixty *seconds* = one minute. Sixty *minutes* = one hour. Twenty-four *hours* = one day. Seven *days* = one *week*.

16 **e.** We *read books*. They have *titles*. We borrow books from *a library*.

17 **e.** Bicycles have *pedals*. When you drive a car your *feet* are on the pedals.

18 **a.** *Fearless* = without *fear*, unafraid. *To fear* = to think something bad is going to happen, to have fear. *Feared* = was afraid (he feared to go).

19 **e.** *Food* [fuːd] is different. *Wood* [wud], *good* [gud], *should* [ʃud] and *could* [kud] have the same sound.

20 **d.** *Fighting* often means *pushing, pulling* and *hurting* someone, as well as *hitting* him.

Unit ten

1 **a.** *A bunch* = a group of small things, usually touching.

2 **b.** The opposite of *hard* = soft. The opposite of *shiny* = dull. The opposite of *sharp* = blunt. *Silky* = soft and shiny (silky hair).

3 **a.** All the others are the most important men: the *leader* of an orchestra, of a gang; the *head* of a company, of a school; the *governor* of a prison. The *boss* = (slang) the most important man, often of a company.

4 **c.** *Working the car* and *operating the car* are not good English.

5 **a.** *A zebra crossing* = a place marked with black and white stripes where people can cross the street safely. (A zebra is an animal like a horse with black and white stripes.)

6 **e.** We *spend money* when we *buy* things and *pay* for them.

7 **d.** *Soup* = a hot liquid made of meat or vegetables: in Britain it is often the first part of the meal.
8 **d.** We *wash down* cars, horses, etc. We *wash out* dirty marks, mud, etc. To do the *washing* = to wash clothes.
9 **a.** All these are musical instruments. *A horn* is a wind instrument. The others all have strings.
10 **a.** The correct sentence is: *I don't want to meet her anywhere.*
11 **a.** *Blood* = the *red* liquid in our bodies.
12 **d.** *A pillow* = the head-rest we use in bed.
13 **b.** Postmen *carry, deliver, leave* and *bring* letters. They do not usually *lose* them. Also the sentence is wrong. The correct sentence is: *The postman lost a letter.*
14 **a.** *Palm trees* can grow only in the south-west of England.
15 **a.** *A waitress* = a woman or girl who serves food in a restaurant. *A cleaner* cleans shops or offices. *A secretary* works in an office; *a headmistress* in a school; *a nurse* in a hospital.
16 **e.** *White* [wait] is the same as *height* [hait]. *Eight* [eit] and *hate* [heit] are the same. *Feat* [fiːt] and *sleet* [sliːt] are the same.
17 **a**
18 **e.** *A dictionary* = a book which gives the meanings of words. We do not read the others.
19 **e.** *To re-cover* = to cover again, to put a new cover on. *To recover* = to get back. *To uncover* = to take off a cover.
20 **c.** *Just* = only (just me and you); also, fair (a just man). *Almost* = nearly. *Along* = for a distance on. *Lonely* = wanting friends.

Unit eleven

1 **b.** We *take off* clothes. *To take something away* = to take it to another place. *To take something*

in = to take it into another place (to take a library book in). *To take something over* = to take control of it (to take over a shop).

2 **d**

3 **d.** *Ice* = *water* below 0°C. *Steam* = water above 100°C. Shoes are often made of *leather*. Car tyres are made of *rubber*.

4 **b.** The others are wrong.

5 **b.** *A light* usually works by *electricity*. When we *switch on* a light, it makes *shadows*.

6 **d.** *A basement* and *a cellar* = rooms below the ground. *A hall* = the first room inside the door of a house; also, a very large room in a school, castle, etc. *A workshop* = a workroom.

7 **d.** *Wide* = *broad*. *Slim* = *thin* (a slim girl, a slim pen). The opposite of *fat* = thin.

8 **d.** *Take it off me!* = Remove it! (Take this spider off my arm!) The other three are not good English.

9 **c.** *Shone* [ʃɔn] is different. *Stone* [stəun], *phone* [fəun], *bone* [bəun] and *alone* [ə'ləun] have the same sound.

10 **e.** *Child's* = of a child (a child's coat).

11 **c.** *Footwear* = things to wear on the feet.

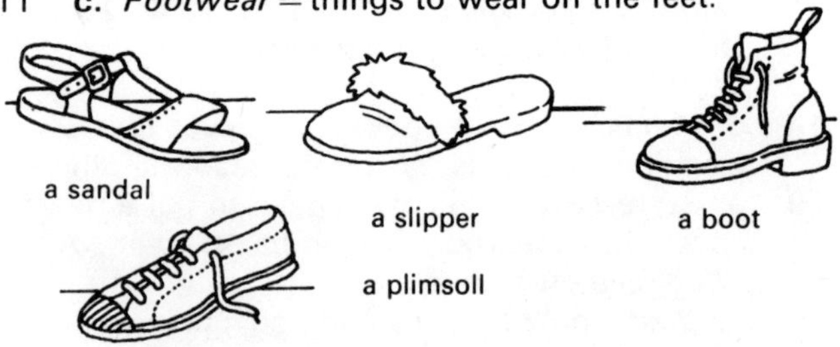

12 **b.** She is wearing a coat. *She's carrying a coat* = The coat is over her arm or in her hand.

13 **c.** The correct sentence is: *I had held the case.*

14 **b.** *A sigh* is *a sound* we make when we *breathe* out in a *sad* way.

15 **b.** *Though* [ðəu] and *show* [ʃəu] have the same sound. *Cough* [kɔf] and *trough* [trɔf] are the same. *Through* [θruː] and *do* [duː] are the same.

16 **a.** *To go in* = to enter. *To go out* = to leave, to exit. *To go down* = to descend.

17 **d.** The opposite of *forward* = backward. The opposite of *to come* = to go. The opposite of *behind* = in front of.

18 **d.** *A cigarette holder* = a small pipe to hold in the teeth when smoking a cigarette. *A cigarette tray* is not English. *An ash-pan* = a holder for taking away the ash in a fireplace. *A cigarette case* = a thin metal case for the pocket to hold cigarettes.

19 **e.** The correct sentence is: *She always invites me, but I never go. Never mind about him* = Don't worry about him.

20 **e.** *To paddle* = to walk in the sea or shallow water for fun. *A hobby* = something we like to do in our free time.

Unit twelve

1 **c.** *A driver* = a person who controls a car. *Headlamps* = the strong lights on the front of a car. *A boot* = the place in a car where the luggage is carried.

2 **a.** *Pain* [pein] and *pane* [pein] sound the same. *Pine* [pain], *pin* [pin], *pan* [pæn] and *pen* [pen] are all different.

3 **e.** *An aeroplane* stands and runs along the ground on its undercarriage.

4 **a**

5 **e.** *A snack* = a light meal eaten at any time. *Breakfast* = the first meal of the day. *Lunch* = the midday meal. *Tea* = a light meal, eaten late afternoon. *Dinner* = an evening meal. (Some

people call the midday meal dinner.)

6 **a.** The opposite of *comfortable* = uncomfortable. The opposite of *smooth* = rough. The opposite of *easy* = difficult. The opposite of *soft* = hard.

7 **c.** We do not say the others.

8 **a.** *A hill* = a low *mountain. A rock* = a large stone (rock = the material which mountains are made of). *A valley* = the lower ground between mountains or hills.

9 **e.** A girl whose name is *Judith* is often called Judy.

10 **d.** The correct sentence is: *Please don't even mention it.*

11 **b.** We put *a film* into *a camera* to take *photographs* We keep photographs in *an album*.

12 **a.** The opposite of *dark* = light.

13 **d.** We do all the other things to letters. The postman *delivers* letters.

14 **d.** This is not good English. We say: *I am hungry*. The others are all correct.

15 **c.** *A cook* prepares food.

16 **c.** *Police* [pəˈliːs] is different. *Please* [pliːz], *knees* [niːz], *cheese* [tʃiːz] and *keys* [kiːz] end with the same sound.

17 **d**

18 **d.** *To get up* = to get out of bed. *To get off* = to leave something you are on. *To get down* = to leave something high. *To get in* = to enter.

19 **a.** In Britain, the *vacation* = the time when universities are closed.

20 **e.** The correct sentence is: *I like swimming*.

Unit thirteen

1 **e.** *He is climbing the wall* = He is going up the wall.

2 **d.** *Your neck* = the part between your head and your body.

3 **d.** *A lake* is usually bigger than *a pool.*

4 **e**

5 **c.** *Honest* = telling the truth. *Just* = fair. *True* = not false; loyal (a true friend). *Well* = healthy.

6 **c.** *Snow* is *cold* and *white* and *falls* from the sky.

7 **a.** The opposite of *thin* = fat (people); thick (things). The opposite of *foolish* = wise. The opposite of *cruel* = kind. The opposite of *weak* = strong.

8 **e.** *A blade* = the part which cuts.

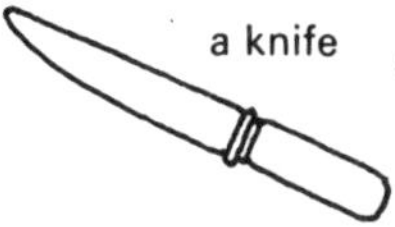

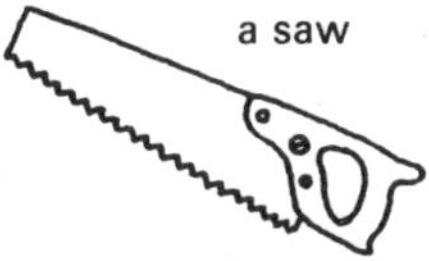

9 **a.** *Fastly* is not an English word. The correct sentence is: *She ran fast.*

10 **d.** *Great* [greit] and *grate* [greit] sound the same. *Grade* [greid] and *greet* [gri:t] are different.

11 **b.** The correct word is: *meeting.*

12 **c.** *A double ticket* = a ticket for two people. The others have no meaning.

13 **a.** The others are not correct.

14 **d.** The opposite of *weak* = strong. The opposite of *long* = short. The opposite of *big* = little. The opposite of *new* = old. Notice: *old* = not new; also, not young.

15 **c.** All the others come from cows.

16 **c**

17 **c.** *Wear* [wɛə] is different. Clear [kliə], *dear* [diə], *near* [niə] and *hear* [hiə] have the same sound.

18 **e.** *You are like it, aren't you* = You look like the food! The others are not good English.

19 **a**

20 **c.** The correct sentence is: *I feel like going dancing.*

Unit fourteen

1 **c.** *A lighthouse* = a tall building with a powerful lamp at the top to guide ships at sea.

2 **d**

3 **a.** When we *tear* our clothes, we can *mend* them with *a needle* and *cotton*.

4 **b.** *A saddle* = the seat on *a horse* or *a bicycle*. *A rider* = somebody who rides on an animal or machine. *A hoof* = an animal's foot. Men who ride on *elephants* do not have saddles.

5 **a.** *Flour* [ˈflauə] is different from *door* [dɔː], *four* [fɔː], *floor* [flɔː] and *more* [mɔː].

6 **a.** *A lid* = a cover which we can move. *Boxes, tins* and *dustbins* have lids which we take off. *An eyelid* = the skin which closes over the *eye*. *Cupboards* have doors.

7 **c.** *Having a bath* = washing in a bath. All the other sentences mean he is swimming.

8 **c.** *Today* = this day.

9 **d.** The others are not good English.

10 **d.** *Filthy* = very *dirty*. The opposite of *wet* = dry. *Muddy* = covered with mud (mud = wet dirt or earth). *Damp* = rather wet.

11 **a.** *To fall asleep = to go to sleep. Asleep = sleeping.*

12 **d.** *Male* [meil] and *mail* [meil] are the same. *Mile* [mail] and *meal* [miːl] are different.

13 **b.** We can *kill* someone by *shooting* him with *a bullet* from *a gun*.

14 **a.** *Brushing* = using a brush (to brush the floor, to brush your hair).

15 **e.** The correct sentence is: *Christmas is always in December.*
16 **b**
17 **d.** *A bus station* = the place where buses stop and start their journeys. The others are not good English.
18 **a.** *Lemonade* has no alcohol in it. *Whisky* has more than *wine* and wine usually has more than *beer*. A strong drink = a drink with a lot of alcohol in it.
19 **c.** *Hard* = not easy; also, not soft.
20 **e.** *A lounge* = *a sitting room* in a house, hotel, ship or pub. *A study* = a room where we read and write.

Unit fifteen

1 **a.** *To throw* = to send from the hand.
2 **b.** *Short* = not long. The opposite of *narrow* = *wide* or *broad*. The opposite of *fat* = *thin*; we talk about thin people, but narrow things (roads, tables).
3 **b**

a hen or a chicken a goose a swan

4 **e.** *Fur* [fəː] has a different sound from *fair* [fɛə], *fare* [fɛə], *hair* [hɛə] and *hare* [hɛə].
5 **a.** The correct sentence is: *I flew there.*
6 **e.** *Redcurrants* grow on a bush. The others grow on trees.
7 **a**
8 **b.** *James* = Jim, Jimmy.
9 **d.** *A greengrocer* sells vegetables and fruit.

A florist sells flowers. *A baker* sells bread.
A grocer sells sugar, cheese, butter, tins of food, and soap.

10 **c.** *Shoelaces* = the strings to fasten shoes.

11 **d.** In *football matches, players* try to score *goals*.

12 **c.** The opposite of *over* = *under*. The opposite of *up* = *down*.

13 **a**

14 **d**

15 **e.** *Paws* [pɔːz] and *pause* [pɔːz] sound the same. *Pose* [pəuz], *pies* [paiz] and *poise* [pɔiz] are different.

16 **b.** *Placing the table* = putting the table in its place. *Making the table* = building the table. The others are not good English.

17 **e.** The opposite of *to begin* = to end. The opposite of *to die* = to live. *To halt* = to stop moving. *To commence* = *to start.*

18 **d.** *He wears spectacles* = He uses spectacles. *He is wearing spectacles* = He has spectacles on now. The other sentences are incorrect.

19 **a**

20 **a.** *A funnel* = a ship's chimney. *A smoker* = someone who smokes. *A steamer* = a kind of ship.

Ihr Testergebnis

Unit one	
Unit two	
Unit three	
Unit four	
Unit five	
Unit six	
Unit seven	
Unit eight	
Unit nine	
Unit ten	
Unit eleven	
Unit twelve	
Unit thirteen	
Unit fourteen	
Unit fifteen	
GESAMT	

Wie geht es weiter?

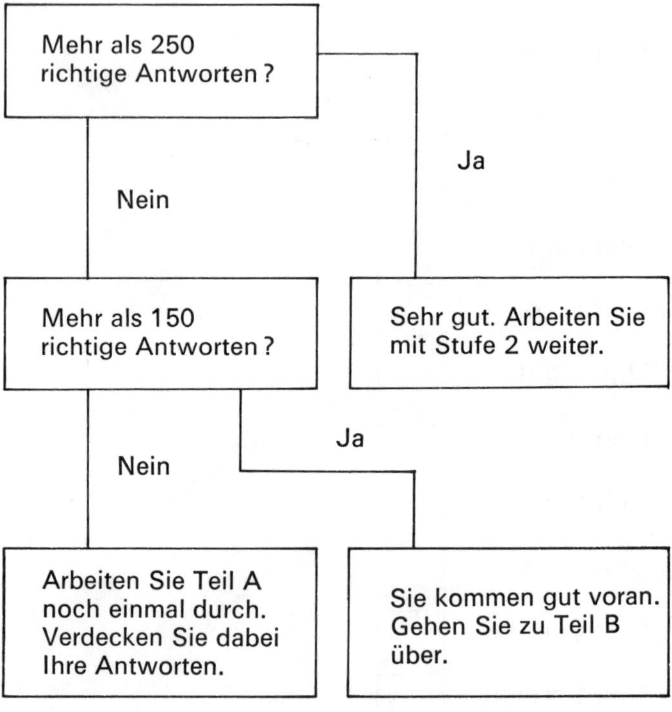

TEIL B

Unit one

1 Which means *two weeks*?

a. a quarter
b. a fortnight
c. a season
d. a weekend
e. a month

2 Which word does not go with all the others?

a. the sky
b. the moon
c. to shine
d. soon
e. night

3 Which is not true?

a. There are two windows upstairs.
b. There's a path to the house.
c. It's raining.
d. The house is among the trees.
e. The clouds are low.

4 Which word does not go with all the others?
a. a policeman
b. a law
c. a helmet
d. a station
e. a train

5 Which word has a different sound?
a. four
b. your
c. more
d. pour
e. hour

6 What do you do to a door with a key?
a. bolt it
b. lock it
c. fasten it
d. close it
e. shut it

7 *See* is to *eyes* as *hear* is to
a. hand
b. head
c. ears
d. mouth
e. nose

8 This man is
a. fat
b. deep
c. thick
d. wide
e. square

9 Which grow in Britain?

a. raspberries
b. bananas
c. lemons
d. oranges
e. pineapples

10 Which means nearly the same as *to hit*?

a. to knock
b. a hand
c. to cry
d. to shout
e. to have

11 What is a wood?

a. a lot of sticks
b. a lot of grass
c. a lot of bushes
d. a lot of trees
e. a lot of flowers

12 Which two words sound the same?

a. mail, mile
b. mail, male
c. mile, mill
d. meal, mill
e. male, mile

13 Which is not true?

a. The driver wasn't in his seat.
b. The passenger was a lady.
c. The doors were open.
d. It was a small car.
e. The driver was getting petrol.

14 Which of these can you not see?

a. a ceiling
b. an eye
c. glass
d. water
e. air

15 Which word does not go with all the others?

a. paint
b. a brush
c. to colour
d. an overcoat
e. to put on

16 The opposite of *few* is

a. much
b. more
c. most
d. many
e. little

17 What is this man?

a. a fisherman
b. a fish man
c. a fishmonger
d. a fishing man
e. a fisher

18 Which of these does not usually have a handle?

a. a case
b. a bucket
c. a drawer
d. a door
e. a bicycle

19 Modern houses usually have . . . cupboards.
a. fitted
b. unfit
c. fitting
d. fit
e. unfitting

20 Which is wrong?
a. What did you say just now?
b. You will finish just in time.
c. I am just going to walk to the corner.
d. He managed to catch just it.
e. I will do just that and nothing else.

Unit two

1 Distance tells us
a. how fast
b. how many
c. how far
d. how much
e. how long

2 Which word does not go with all the others?
a. to think
b. ideas
c. to wonder
d. head
e. good

3 Which of these can you not carry?
a. a lorry
b. a rifle
c. clothes
d. a jug
e. a ticket

4 What is this?
a. a lift
b. a climber
c. a stair
d. a step
e. a ladder

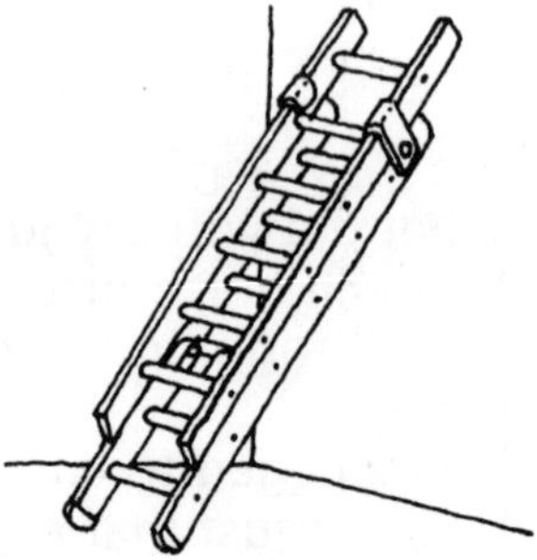

5 Which two words sound the same?
a. bear, bare
b. beer, bear
c. bar, bear
d. beer, bare
e. bar, bare

6 Which means *to enter*?
a. to appear
b. to begin
c. to open
d. to go in
e. to go

7 What is he doing to the dog?
a. kicking it
b. touching it
c. hitting it
d. knocking it
e. banging it

8 Which of these is not an insect?
a. a fly
b. an ant
c. a mosquito
d. a bee
e. a snake

9 Which word does not go with all the others?
a. a telephone
b. to ring
c. a knocker
d. to answer
e. to call

10 Which word sounds the same as *purse*?
a. worse
b. hours
c. course
d. horse
e. pours

11 Which means *recently*?
a. before
b. then
c. soon
d. lately
e. late

12 Which word does not go with all the others?
a. music
b. a purse
c. money
d. a note
e. a wallet

13 The opposite of *deep* is
a. thick
b. narrow
c. thin
d. wide
e. shallow

14 What is she waving?
a. a sheet
b. a handkerchief
c. a towel
d. a cloth
e. a carpet

15 Which means *very busy*?
a. in good hands
b. lending a hand
c. out of hand
d. having your hands full
e. shaking hands

16 Which is not a metal?
a. iron
b. steel
c. gold
d. glass
e. silver

17 Which word means the same as *nasty*?
a. no
b. beautiful
c. ugly
d. horrible
e. nice

18 What is this man?
a. a policeman
b. a soldier
c. a doctor
d. a dentist
e. a nurse

19 *Big* is to *little* as *difficult* is to
a. hard
b. easy
c. light
d. dark
e. right

20 Which word describes all the others?
a. a car
b. a vehicle
c. a bicycle
d. a scooter
e. a bus

Unit three

1 Which of these is black?
a. a flame
b. silver
c. a fire
d. coal
e. wood

2 What is the opposite of *long*?
a. tiny
b. thin
c. small
d. short
e. low

3 Which is not true?
a. He's drinking.
b. He's behind the chair.
c. He's not in bed.
d. The chair's behind him.
e. He's standing up.

4 If you call a man Andy, his name is
a. Anthony
b. Andrew
c. Alan
d. Arthur
e. Albert

5 Which has wings?
a. a mouse
b. a pig
c. a rabbit
d. a fish
e. a chicken

6 Which of these can you climb?
a. a horse
b. a hill
c. a plane
d. a chair
e. a field

7 What is this?
a. a lamp
b. a light
c. a lighter
d. a torch
e. lightning

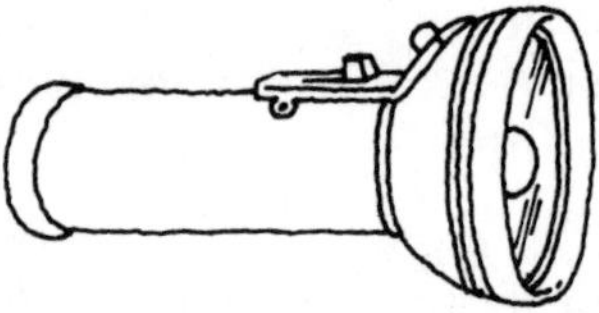

8 Which word has a different sound?
a. palm
b. calm
c. farm
d. warm
e. harm

9 If someone asks, *Why did you go?*, you might answer, *I don't know why I*
a. goes
b. goed
c. went
d. gone
e. go

10 In which sentence does *give up* mean *stop*?

a. Try to give up smoking.
b. Give up your ticket at the gate.
c. He gave up his seat to a lady.
d. The thief gave himself up to the police.
e. I don't know the answer: I give up.

11 When we want things to go right for someone, we say

a. Good luck!
b. Good fortune!
c. Good chance!
d. Good opportunity!
e. Good possibility!

12 What is she doing to the glove?

a. taking it
b. picking it
c. holding it
d. holding it up
e. picking it up

13 What does a camper live in?

a. a barn
b. a haystack
c. a hut
d. a tent
e. a sleeping bag

14 Which word rhymes with *allow*?
a. follow
b. widow
c. fellow
d. rough
e. plough

15 Which word does not go with all the others?
a. an arm
b. a cuff
c. a sleeve
d. a wrist
e. a knee

16 The opposite of *beginning* is
a. death
b. finish
c. close
d. end
e. stop

17 Which means *unsafe*?
a. hurt
b. damage
c. unsure
d. dangerous
e. uncertain

18 Which word means nearly the same as *modern*?
a. tomorrow
b. today
c. young
d. old
e. new

19 Which word does not go with all the others?
a. to carry
b. water
c. sea
d. a drop
e. to wash

20 What is he doing?
   a. listening the radio
   b. hearing the radio
   c. listening to the radio
   d. earing the radio
   e. attending to the radio

Unit four

1 Which is not true?
   a. It's a chilly day.
   b. It's a sunny day.
   c. He's sunbathing.
   d. He's facing the sun.
   e. There are some flowers behind him.

2 Which of these colours is also a fruit?

a. orange
b. white
c. brown
d. blue
e. pink

3 Which is incorrect?

a. He received the bill.
b. He read the bill.
c. He added up the bill.
d. He payed the bill.
e. He threw the bill away.

4 Which is a boy's name?

a. Angela
b. Helen
c. George
d. Elizabeth
e. Anne

5 Which has feathers?

a. a dog
b. a cat
c. a pig
d. a fish
e. a bird

6 Which word does not go with all the others?

a. a letter
b. a stamp
c. to post
d. to read
e. a foot

7 This man is

a. a conductor
b. a guide
c. a pilot
d. a chauffeur
e. a driver

8 Which means *to permit*?

a. to push
b. to help
c. to persuade
d. to encourage
e. to allow

9 The opposite of *to fill* is

a. to empty
b. to remove
c. to take out
d. to lower
e. to shut

10 Which of these is green?

a. leather
b. a flowerpot
c. cheese
d. grass
e. the sky

11 What does a small child call a tick-tock?

a. a train
b. a car
c. a clock
d. a bicycle
e. a ball

12 Which word has a different sound?

a. shout
b. coat
c. wrote
d. boat
e. note

13 Which word means the same as *happy*?

a. miserable
b. funny
c. comfortable
d. glad
e. sad

14 Which is not true?

a. Six passengers have arrived.
b. The driver has not got in.
c. Some passengers have sat down.
d. The passengers are all sitting.
e. The bus isn't moving.

15 What does an Englishman usually say?

a. North, East, West, South
b. North, South, East, West
c. East, South, North, West
d. West, East, North, South
e. South, North, West, East

16 What is the opposite of *lying down*?
a. standing
b. lying
c. standing up
d. sitting down
e. falling over

17 What do you say if your watch is broken?
a. It's unworkable.
b. It is without work.
c. It doesn't work.
d. It is hard-working.
e. It's working.

18 Where are the eggs?
a. in a nut
b. in a nest
c. in a knot
d. in the next
e. in a net

19 Which word has a different sound?
a. ice
b. mice
c. rice
d. practice
e. twice

20 *Sun* is to *day* as *moon* is to
a. night
b. morning
c. week
d. afternoon
e. month

Unit five

1 Which of these is not a building?
a. a house
b. a church
c. a school
d. a tent
e. a shop

2 Which word does not go with all the others?
a. fire
b. to tear
c. smoke
d. to burn
e. heat

3 What is he saying?
a. I can't pick up it.
b. I can't to pick it up.
c. I can't picked it up.
d. I can't picking it up.
e. I can't pick it up.

4 The opposite of *fast* is
a. slow
b. unmoving
c. still
d. quiet
e. quick

5 Which word describes all the others?

a. a chair
b. a sofa
c. a stool
d. a seat
e. a settee

6 *Hand* is to *finger* as *foot* is to

a. toe
b. finger
c. leg
d. arm
e. thumb

7 Which is not true?

a. Here is a spider.
b. The spider has made a web.
c. Spiders catch flies.
d. The spider is in the middle of the web.
e. A fly has been caught in the web.

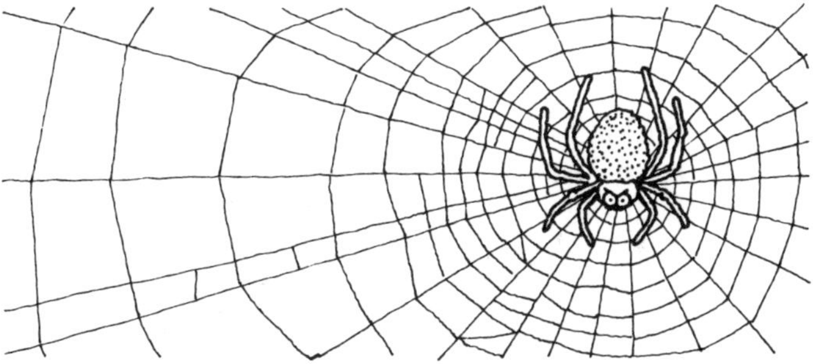

8 What colour is a daffodil?

a. yellow
b. orange
c. white
d. red
e. blue

9 Where does a mechanic work?
a. on a bus
b. in a garage
c. in an office
d. in a hotel
e. in a nightclub

10 Where do we wear a belt?
a. round the neck
b. round the arm
c. round the wrist
d. round the waist
e. round the leg

11 Which word does not go with all the others?
a. number
b. to count
c. to add
d. arithmetic
e. an adder

12 What is she sitting on?
a. a fence
b. a wall
c. a gate
d. an entrance
e. a door

13 Which two words sound the same?
a. board, boat
b. bored, boat
c. bored, board
d. bored, bought
e. bought, boat

14 Which word means *cheap*?
a. to pay
b. to buy
c. inexpensive
d. money
e. expensive

15 The opposite of *the bottom* is
a. the front
b. the side
c. the end
d. the middle
e. the top

16 What do you give someone when you are angry with him?
a. a black book
b. a blacklist
c. a black pudding
d. a black look
e. a blackboard

17 You can see a long way into the distance when the air is
a. a clearing
b. cleared
c. a clearance
d. unclear
e. clear

18 Which word has a different sound?
a. bead
b. said
c. head
d. dead
e. bread

19 What are these?
a. lighters
b. stop lights
c. traffic lights
d. traffic lamps
e. car lights

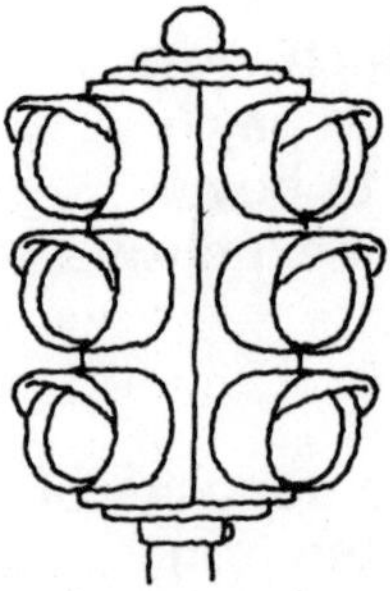

20 Which of these is lightest?
a. coal
b. ice
c. petrol
d. water
e. air

Unit six

1 Which means nearly the same as *a game*?
a. to watch
b. a sport
c. a football
d. to play
e. work

2 Which two words sound the same?
a. floor, flour
b. flew, flower
c. flow, floor
d. flour, flower
e. flier, flew

3 In which sentence does *drop off* mean *go to sleep*?
   a. My button dropped off.
   b. Tired drivers sometimes drop off at the wheel.
   c. Drop me off on the corner.
   d. In the summer, umbrella sales drop off.
   e. Apples often drop off trees.

4 What is the opposite of *most*?
   a. few
   b. less
   c. little
   d. some
   e. least

5 She is taking a photograph
   a. to the children
   b. by the children
   c. from the children
   d. of the children
   e. with the children

6 We put a letter in

a. a paper
b. a packet
c. a parcel
d. a paper bag
e. an envelope

7 Which word does not go with all the others?

a. a piano
b. to play
c. music
d. to lock
e. keys

8 What is she holding?

a. a cup
b. a jug
c. a dish
d. a jar
e. a glass

9 Which word describes a dead body?

a. lively
b. alive
c. living
d. lifeless
e. liveliness

10 Which is not part of your face?

a. the nose
b. the eyes
c. the eyebrows
d. the thigh
e. the mouth

11 Which man does not work in a shop?
a. a tobacconist
b. an artist
c. a barber
d. a grocer
e. a butcher

12 *Boy* is to *son* as *girl* is to
a. child
b. wife
c. sister
d. daughter
e. mother

13 What is this?
a. a ladybird
b. a frog
c. a beetle
d. a lizard
e. a worm

14 Which is wrong?
a. I drink tea.
b. You are drinking tea.
c. She drank tea.
d. He drinks tea.
e. They have dranked their tea.

15 Which do we not buy at the butcher's?
a. a joint
b. a chop
c. mince
d. stew
e. sausages

16 Which word has a different sound?

a. stirred
b. bird
c. hired
d. word
e. heard

17 Which word does not go with all the others?

a. clothes
b. body
c. to wear
d. humans
e. animals

18 What is he carrying?

a. a pin
b. a bone
c. a bar
d. a rod
e. a stick

19 Which is different?

a. to watch
b. to listen
c. to look
d. to see
e. to stare

20 Which of these can you not close?

a. your eyes
b. your hand
c. a pencil
d. a case
e. a door

Unit seven

1 Which part of a phone do you speak into?
   a. a phone box
   b. a receiver
   c. an operator
   d. a directory
   e. a phone call

2 Which do we use to tie up boats?
   a. cotton
   b. thread
   c. rope
   d. string
   e. cord

3 Which is wrong?
   a. He's on the telephone.
   b. He's having a telephone.
   c. He's using the telephone.
   d. He's having a telephone conversation.
   e. He's telephoning.

4 What is the opposite of *never*?
a. once
b. immediately
c. always
d. often
e. early

5 Which word rhymes with *grey*?
a. day
b. key
c. quay
d. free
e. dye

6 Which speaker is a thief?
a. I accepted some money.
b. I received some money.
c. I acquired some money.
d. I gained some money.
e. I stole some money.

7 What is this?
a. a timetable
b. a calendar
c. a date
d. a notice
e. a diary

8 When you buy some wallpaper, what are you going to do with it?
a. put it on the wall
b. clean the wall
c. make a parcel
d. draw a wall
e. read it

9 Which of these can cut things?
a. water
b. a fire
c. scissors
d. paper
e. a hammer

10 Which is a girl's name?
a. Henry
b. Charles
c. James
d. Jane
e. Robert

11 Which is different from all the others?
a. a circle
b. a square
c. an oval
d. a street
e. a triangle

12 Which has a beak?
a. a bird
b. a dog
c. a rabbit
d. a fish
e. a fly

13 What is the boy saying?
a. Throw!
b. Have!
c. Take!
d. Get!
e. Catch!

14 Which is wrong?
a. I want to have my hair cut.
b. She cuts my hair.
c. He cut my hair.
d. I have cut my own hair.
e. You are cuting my hair.

15 The opposite of *ugly* is
a. uglier
b. more beautiful
c. nice
d. beautiful
e. sweet

16 Which word has a different sound?
a. all
b. shall
c. tall
d. call
e. hall

17 Where is her scarf?
a. with her neck
b. in her neck
c. at her neck
d. on her neck
e. round her neck

18 Which word has nothing to do with all the others?
a. a dance
b. a businessman
c. a meeting
d. a report
e. an office

19 Which is a piece of paper and also part of a tree?
- a. leaf
- b. sheet
- c. page
- d. trunk
- e. bill

20 Which means *staying calm*?
- a. putting your heads together
- b. keeping your head
- c. losing your head
- d. coming to a head
- e. biting someone's head off

Unit eight

1 What is this?
- a. a slipper
- b. a shoe
- c. a boot
- d. a sandal
- e. a sock

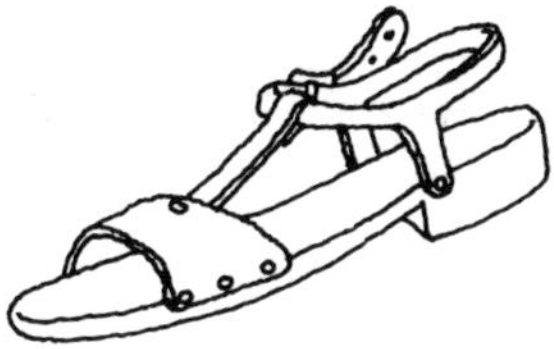

2 The opposite of *to fasten* is
- a. to close
- b. to shut
- c. to open
- d. to break
- e. to unfasten

3 Which of these is the largest?
a. a river
b. an ocean
c. a stream
d. a lake
e. a sea

4 John married Mary. Mary's mother is Alice. Alice is John's
a. mother
b. mother-in-law
c. sister
d. foster mother
e. stepmother

5 Which word means *to anger*?
a. to trouble
b. to annoy
c. to fight
d. to chase
e. to frighten

6 Where do you wear a beret?
a. on your head
b. round your shoulders
c. round your waist
d. on your feet
e. round your neck

7 What do we carry in a purse?
a. cigarettes
b. papers
c. money
d. tobacco
e. food

8 Which word does not go with all the others?
a. a clock
b. fingers
c. hands
d. time
e. hours

9 What is he doing?
a. skiing
b. walking
c. skating
d. sliding
e. slipping

10 Which means *to memorise*?
a. learning by heart
b. having a change of heart
c. breaking your heart
d. having your heart in your mouth
e. taking heart

11 Another word for *twelve* is
a. a score
b. a dozen
c. a pair
d. a gross
e. a century

12 Which word means *centre*?
a. end
b. middle
c. half
d. top
e. beginning

13 Which is correct?

a. Were are you?
b. Wear are you?
c. Air are you?
d. Where are you?
e. Here are you?

14 Which two words sound the same?

a. fire, fair
b. fir, fire
c. fare, far
d. fair, fare
e. fear, fare

15 The opposite of *arrive* is

a. come
b. go
c. arrived
d. depart
e. left

16 What is she doing?

a. bending
b. kneeling
c. standing
d. sitting
e. kneeing

17 Which word has a different sound?
a. their
b. there
c. they're
d. were
e. where

18 A husband and wife are
a. marry
b. married
c. marrying
d. marries
e. marryed

19 Where does an usherette work?
a. in an aeroplane
b. on a ship
c. in a cinema
d. in a museum
e. in a station

20 If you have an accident, you may be
a. painful
b. in pain
c. pained
d. pain
e. paining

Unit nine

1 The opposite of *to forget* is
a. to remember
b. to discover
c. to find
d. to know
e. to think

2 Which is wrong?
   a. They go by theirselves.
   b. Don't hurt yourself.
   c. She talks to herself.
   d. I was angry with myself.
   e. We enjoyed ourselves.

3 Speed tells us
   a. how fast
   b. how much
   c. how many
   d. how long
   e. how far

4 What is she wearing?
   a. a watch
   b. glasses
   c. a spectator
   d. a spectacle
   e. a glass

5 The words *feather, tail* and *wing* all have something to do with
   a. aeroplanes
   b. birds
   c. brushes
   d. animals
   e. coats

6 Which word has a different sound?
   a. cool
   b. school
   c. fool
   d. you'll
   e. wool

7 Which of these is not a colour?

a. black
b. green
c. yellow
d. red
e. blew

8 What is he doing?

a. dropping
b. descending
c. falling
d. going down
e. coming down

9 If you call a girl Katy, her name is

a. Christine
b. Carol
c. Clare
d. Catherine
e. Charlotte

10 Which word describes all the others?

a. milk
b. wine
c. paraffin
d. liquid
e. lemonade

11 Which word does not go with all the others?

a. a voice
b. to frown
c. a conversation
d. to whisper
e. to sing

12 What is the opposite of *to give*?

a. to sell
b. to carry
c. to bring
d. to take
e. to have

13 Two people sitting right next to each other are sitting

a. side to side
b. side touching side
c. side against side
d. side up to side
e. side by side

14 Which is not true?

a. The spoon is shorter than the knife.
b. The plate is above the spoon.
c. The fork is shorter than the knife.
d. The knife is the longest.
e. The plate is below the spoon.

15 Which word rhymes with *praise*?

a. face
b. gaze
c. prize
d. prise
e. price

16 Which of these can you play?

a. a film
b. a television
c. a radio
d. a trumpet
e. a hammer

17 What is this?

a. a heater
b. an aircraft
c. a cooler
d. a fan
e. a propeller

18 Which means *to help*?

a. to call
b. to add
c. to consist of
d. to insist
e. to assist

19 Which word means *a piece*?

a. half
b. small
c. many
d. a bit
e. a lot

20 Which word does not go with all the others?

a. head
b. a page
c. hat
d. to wear
e. size

Unit ten

1 Where do you see an announcer?
a. on television
b. in a newspaper office
c. in a factory
d. in a solicitor's office
e. in a college

2 What is the opposite of *to lend*?
a. to buy
b. to sell
c. to steal
d. to borrow
e. to give

3 Which is wrong?
a. He's thoughtful.
b. He's thinking.
c. He's a deep thinker.
d. He's having a think.
e. He's thoughtish.

4 Which word means *silly*?
a. to laugh
b. foolish
c. untrue
d. intelligent
e. clever

5 Which word does not go with all the others?

a. a pool
b. to swim
c. water
d. wet
e. a cup

6 Which word has the same sound as *above*?

a. move
b. stove
c. drove
d. wove
e. love

7 You can use a brush to do all these things, except one.

a. tidy your hair
b. clean your teeth
c. mend a sock
d. clean the floor
e. paint a door

8 What is this?

a. a dam
b. a lid
c. a cork
d. a shutter
e. a plug

9 Which word does not go with all the others?

a. a knife
b. empty
c. a blade
d. to cut
e. sharp

10 Beef is meat from
a. a sheep
b. a chicken
c. a horse
d. a pig
e. a cow

11 Which of these is fastest?
a. a bicycle
b. a car
c. a boat
d. a train
e. a plane

12 What is she saying?
a. I don't drink it never!
b. I drink never it!
c. I never drink it!
d. Never I drink it!
e. I drink it never!

13 When a child calls *Daddy*, he wants his
a. grandfather
b. sister
c. father
d. brother
e. mother

14 When an aeroplane leaves the ground it
a. takes up
b. takes away
c. takes on
d. takes above
e. takes off

15 Which is wrong?
a. He also never eats meat.
b. He hates meat and also cheese.
c. He is also not very fond of fish.
d. He does not like also eggs.
e. He hates milk also.

16 Which word is nearest to *sure*?
a. to know
b. certain
c. yes
d. unsure
e. uncertain

17 What is he saying?
a. Them give to me!
b. Me them give!
c. Give them to me!
d. Me give them!
e. Them me give!

18 Which word does not go with all the others?
a. a restaurant
b. to eat
c. food
d. a waiter
e. happy

19 What is the opposite of *true*?
a. incorrect
b. false
c. wrong
d. faulty
e. faithful

20 Which of these things is not usually round?
a. a wheel
b. a record
c. a ball
d. a stamp
e. a tin

Unit eleven

1 Which word has a different sound?
a. placed
b. waste
c. raised
d. raced
e. waist

2 What is she doing?

a. telling her watch
b. looking at her watch
c. looking her watch
d. looking for her watch
e. seeing her watch

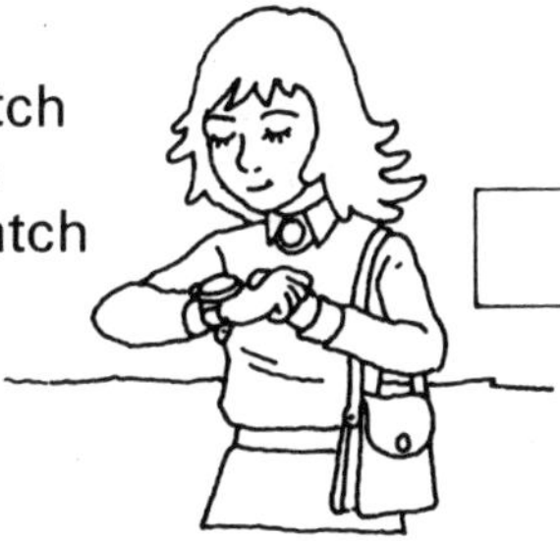

3 If you call a man Ted, his name is

a. Thomas
b. Terence
c. Frederick
d. William
e. Edward

4 Which do you not catch?

a. a fish
b. a bus
c. a cold
d. a headache
e. a ball

5 What animal do young children sometimes call a bow-wow?

a. a tortoise
b. a monkey
c. a horse
d. a dog
e. a cow

6 Which word does not go with all the others?

a. to move
b. to drink
c. to wash
d. to sail
e. to float

7 We see films in a cinema, but what do we see in a theatre?

a. films
b. acts
c. music
d. plays
e. scenes

8 These children are the teacher's

a. students
b. scholars
c. learners
d. beginners
e. pupils

9 What do barbers do?

a. cut men's hair
b. make fences
c. sell fish
d. work in a bank
e. make clothes

10 Which two words sound the same?

a. would, word
b. wood, word
c. word, world
d. world, would
e. would, wood

11 Where do you put a cup?

a. on a pan
b. on a glass
c. on a dish
d. on a plate
e. on a saucer

12 What is the opposite of *quick*?
a. fast
b. slow
c. silent
d. rapid
e. unmoving

13 Which do we not say?
a. He was sleeping fast.
b. He was driving fast.
c. He was running fast.
d. He was thinking fast.
e. He was learning fast.

14 Which is wrong?
a. Put out it.
b. Put your tongue out.
c. Put out your tongue.
d. Put it out.
e. Show me your tongue.

15 Which can't you travel in?
a. a train
b. a car
c. a bus
d. a plane
e. a bicycle

16 What is this?
a. a fountain
b. a river
c. a pool
d. a drop of water
e. a waterfall

17 Which word does not go with all the others?
a. a curtain
b. to cover
c. a handle
d. a window
e. to draw

18 Which answer means *a pair*?
a. half
b. a dozen
c. one
d. a couple
e. a twin

19 The opposite of *behind* is
a. under
b. over
c. next to
d. near
e. in front of

20 Who works in a hospital?
a. a sailor
b. a builder
c. a nurse
d. a headmistress
e. a salesman

Unit twelve

1 Which insect gives honey?
a. a bee
b. an ant
c. a mosquito
d. a butterfly
e. a wasp

2 He's asking: *How are you going*? What is the answer?

a. With a plane.
b. By plane.
c. With plane.
d. In plane.
e. On plane.

3 *Son* is to *daughter* as *nephew* is to

a. niece
b. sister
c. daughter
d. aunt
e. grandmother

4 Which word does not go with all the others?

a. to sell
b. a shop
c. a customer
d. an assistant
e. aid

5 Which of these means *immediately*?

a. presently
b. before long
c. shortly
d. soon
e. at once

6 Which of these is biggest?
a. a field
b. a country
c. a village
d. a city
e. a town

7 Which of these is dangerous?
a. a pig
b. a cow
c. a horse
d. a cat
e. a lion

8 What is he doing to the wood?
a. sawing it
b. splitting it
c. opening it
d. hitting it
e. breaking it

9 We say one *sheep*, but two
a. sheep's
b. sheep
c. sheeps
d. sheepen
e. sheeps'

10 A policeman is an . . . of the law.
a. office
b. official
c. unofficial
d. officer
e. offices

11 Which word has a different sound?

a. showed
b. broad
c. rowed
d. road
e. toad

12 Which word usually completes this phrase: pots and

a. saucepans
b. kettles
c. money
d. potatoes
e. pans

13 This bird is in

a. a basket
b. a cage
c. a box
d. a case
e. a nest

14 What is the opposite of *new*?

a. ancient
b. old
c. worn out
d. adult
e. young

15 A date is a certain day of a certain month. It can also be

a. an address on a letter
b. a fruit
c. a song
d. a hat
e. a gift

16 Which word does not go with all the others?
a. a bath
b. a shower
c. rain
d. to fall
e. a mackintosh

17 Which means *hurrying*?
a. on the move
b. making a move
c. moving in
d. moving up
e. getting a move on

18 Which is correct?
a. The vase breaks.
b. The vase is breaking.
c. The vase is broken.
d. The vase broken.
e. The vase was breaking.

19 *Important* is to *unimportant* as *useful* is to
a. useless
b. unuseful
c. disuseful
d. inuseful
e. nonuseful

20 Which comes just before night?
a. evening
b. black
c. afternoon
d. day
e. morning

Unit thirteen

1 Which of these is soft?
a. rock
b. ice
c. metal
d. wood
e. fur

2 All these are games, which is not a ball game?
a. football
b. tennis
c. hockey
d. badminton
e. rugby

3 What is she doing?
a. washing the face
b. washing her face
c. washing face
d. washing a face
e. washing the faces

4 Where do you go to see your doctor?
a. to his office
b. to his surgery
c. to his shop
d. to his showroom
e. to his hotel

5 Who looks after a building at night?
a. a watchman
b. a watch
c. watchful
d. unwatched
e. a watcher

6 How do we usually say this date: 1980?
a. One nine eighty
b. nineteen hundred and eighty
c. one thousand, nine hundred and eighty
d. one nine eight nought
e. nineteen eighty

7 Which word does not go with all the others?
a. a wedding
b. a bride
c. to marry
d. a cinema
e. a church

8 Which word has a different sound?
a. thought
b. court
c. ought
d. spot
e. sport

9 The opposite of *far* is
- a. near
- b. here
- c. nearly
- d. next
- e. closed

10 He cannot
- a. see
- b. regard
- c. look at
- d. look
- e. watch

11 What does a butcher sell?
- a. newspapers
- b. fruit
- c. milk
- d. meat
- e. vegetables

12 Which part of a room is over your head?
- a. the door
- b. the window
- c. the wall
- d. the floor
- e. the ceiling

13 What is this?
- a. a match
- b. a candle
- c. a fire
- d. a light
- e. a lamp

14 Which tells where you live?
a. a dress
b. your home
c. your house
d. your address
e. your desk

15 Which two words sound the same?
a. scent, sent
b. cent, cant
c. scant, cant
d. saint, scent
e. cent, send

16 Which word does not go with all the others?
a. to play
b. to sing
c. a song
d. a voice
e. music

17 What is this?
a. a fountain pen
b. a crayon
c. a pencil
d. chalk
e. a ball-point pen

18 The opposite of *empty* is
a. high
b. closed
c. full
d. shut
e. filled

19 Which of these can you eat?
a. paper
b. plastic
c. beer
d. a biscuit
e. whisky

☐

20 Which means *out-of-date*?
a. beating time
b. behind the times
c. on time
d. in no time
e. keeping good time

☐

Unit fourteen

1 Which word does not go with all the others?
a. tears
b. to cry
c. eyes
d. sad
e. a cough

☐

2 Which two words sound the same?
a. night, neat
b. knit, knight
c. night, knit
d. knight, night
e. knit, neat

☐

3 Where is she putting her purse?
a. in a bucket
b. in a basket
c. in a bottle
d. in a bowl
e. in a bag

4 Which is wrong?
a. I sleep well at night.
b. Have you slept well?
c. He sleeps well too.
d. I sleeped all morning.
e. She is still sleeping.

5 Which of these is hot?
a. coal
b. wool
c. rain
d. a day
e. a fire

6 *Pork* is to *pig* as *mutton* is to
a. beef
b. deer
c. sheep
d. calf
e. cow

7 What is this?
a. a disc
b. a zip
c. a buckle
d. a fastener
e. a button

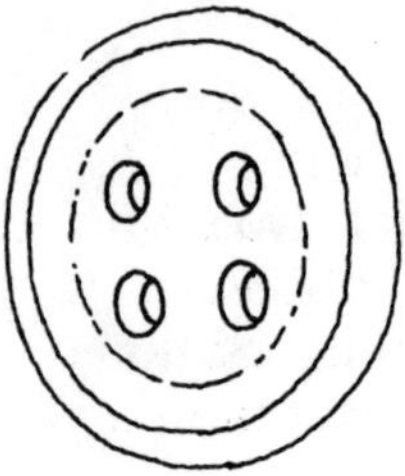

8 Which of these is heaviest?
a. plastic
b. iron
c. glass
d. rubber
e. paper

9 Weight tells us
a. how high
b. how cold
c. how heavy
d. how often
e. how big

10 Which is different from all the others?
a. twice
b. a pair
c. two
d. brothers
e. twins

11 Which word has nothing to do with hospitals?
a. a nurse
b. a patient
c. ill
d. medicine
e. a night club

12 Which is wrong?
a. His leg looked painfully.
b. He shouted angrily.
c. She swam strongly.
d. We dropped it accidentally.
e. They sang sweetly.

13 What is he doing?
a. colouring
b. painting
c. brushing
d. writing
e. drawing

☐

14 The opposite of *clean* is
a. dirty
b. dark
c. untidy
d. black
e. bad

☐

15 *Fall* is the American word for
a. autumn
b. spring
c. summer
d. winter
e. midnight

☐

16 Which word usually goes with *knife*?
a. spoon
b. fork
c. cup
d. plate
e. napkin

☐

17 What is she saying?
a. I want to go back!
b. I'm wanting back!
c. I'm wanting going back!
d. I want going back!
e. I want back!

☐

18 Which means the same as *a tin*?
a. a packet
b. a bag
c. a can
d. a case
e. a box

☐

19 Which of these is longest?
a. an hour
b. a week
c. a year
d. a season
e. a month

☐

20 What is the opposite of *off*?
a. out
b. over
c. under
d. through
e. on

☐

Unit fifteen

1 The opposite of *a friend* is
a. a boss
b. a slave
c. an enemy
d. a neighbour
e. a pal

2 Which means *a shock*?
a. a party
b. a meeting
c. an impolite person
d. a bar of chocolate
e. a nasty surprise

3 This girl has long
a. eyelids
b. eyebrows
c. eye sockets
d. eyeballs
e. eyelashes

4 Which word does not go with all the others?
a. a scarf
b. a paw
c. an animal
d. a mane
e. a coat

5 Which word has the same sound as *flow*?
a. bough
b. through
c. thaw
d. zoo
e. hoe

6 Which do we not wear on our feet?
a. socks
b. belts
c. stockings
d. shoes
e. boots

7 Which word has nothing to do with school?
a. a prison
b. a blackboard
c. a teacher
d. a classroom
e. a pupil

8 What is she doing?
a. flying
b. diving
c. swimming
d. jumping
e. falling

9 When you argue with someone you . . . with him.
a. disagree
b. agreement
c. disagreeable
d. agree
e. agreed

10 *River* is to *bank* as *sea* is to
a. land
b. edge
c. shore
d. shell
e. sand

11 Which do we not say?
a. He received a telephone call.
b. He received happiness.
c. He received a reward.
d. He received a smack on the hand.
e. He received his sister with a smile.

12 If you call a boy Dick, his name is
a. Dennis
b. Alan
c. Roger
d. Arthur
e. Richard

13 What is the opposite of *to push*?
a. to send
b. to pull
c. to bring
d. to put
e. to tow

14 Where are these children playing?
a. in a play garden
b. in a playroom
c. in a plaything
d. in a play square
e. in a playground

15 Which of these can you turn?

a. a corner
b. a year
c. a path
d. a house
e. a letter

16 Which word has a different sound?

a. ride
b. worried
c. died
d. hide
e. inside

17 Which is wrong?

a. He's being helpful.
b. He's a good helper.
c. He's very helpish.
d. His mother is helpless.
e. He's helping.

18 Which can mean *a notice*?

a. to draw
b. a sign
c. to write
d. a wall
e. a picture

19 Where does a cashier work?
- a. in a toolshed
- b. in a kitchen
- c. in a bank
- d. at a swimming pool
- e. in a studio

☐

20 Complete this phrase: bread and
- a. butter
- b. cake
- c. meat
- d. flour
- e. biscuits

☐

Answer section

Answers

Unit one

1 **b.** *A quarter* = three months. *A season* = one of spring, summer, autumn, winter. *A weekend* = Saturday and Sunday. *A month* = a twelfth part of a year: January, February and March are the first three months.
2 **d.** The *moon shines* in the *sky* at *night*.
3 **a**
4 **e.** *Policemen*, who wear *helmets* and work in police *stations*, make people keep the *law*.
5 **e.** *Hour* [ˈauə] is different from *four* [fɔː], *your* [jɔː], *more* [mɔː], and *pour* [pɔː].
6 **b.** *To lock* = *to fasten* with *a key*. *To bolt* = to fasten with a bolt. *To close* = *to shut*.

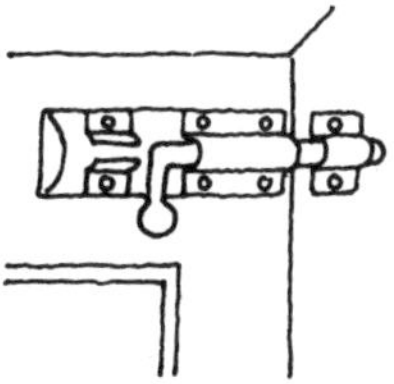

a bolt

7 **c.** We *see* with our *eyes*, and *hear* with our *ears*. We touch with our *hand*, and smell with our *nose*.
8 **a.** When a man is *deep*, he has many secrets. *Thick* = (slang) unintelligent. Things are *wide*, but people are broad. We are unlikely to call a man *square*.
9 **a.** Britain is not warm enough for the other fruit to grow.

10 **a.** I *hit* my head on the door = I *knocked* my head on the door. But notice: I knocked on the door (I wanted to go in); I hit the door (I was angry).

11 **d**

12 **b.** *Mail* and *male* are the same [meil]. *Mile* [mail], *mill* [mil] and *meal* [mi:l] are different.

13 **c**

14 **e**

15 **d.** We use *a brush to put on paint to colour* things. Notice: when we paint wood, we first put on an undercoat, then a top coat. *An overcoat* = a thick coat we wear in cold weather.

16 **d.** The opposite of *much* = *little*. The opposite of *more* = less. The opposite of *most* = least.

17 **a.** *A fishmonger* sells fish in a shop. *A fisher* = (very unusual) a bird or a boat that catches fish. The others are not good English.

18 **e.** *A bicycle* has handlebars. All the others have *handles*.

19 **a.** *Fitted cupboards* = cupboards which are specially made and fixed. *Unfit* = ill. *Fit* = healthy. Notice: cupboards which do not fit well are badly fitting cupboards. The others are wrong.

20 **d.** The correct sentence is: *He just managed to catch it.*

Unit two

1 **c.** Speed tells us *how fast*. Number tells us *how many*. Quantity tells us *how much*. Length tells us *how long*.

2 **e.** We often have *ideas* in our *head* when we *wonder* or *think*.

3 **a**

a lorry

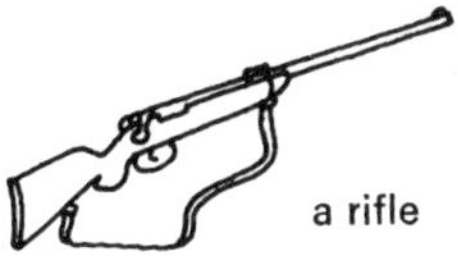

Notice: we can *carry clothes* in our hands, but when we have them on, we are wearing them.

4 **e.** *A lift* = a machine which carries people up and down in a building. *A climber* = a person who climbs.

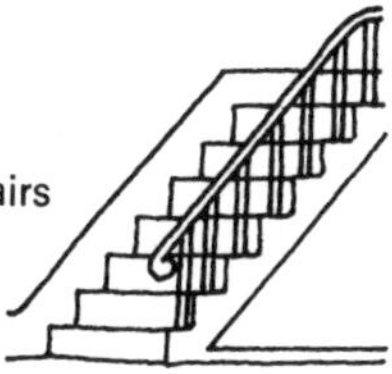

5 **a.** *Bear* and *bare* are the same [bεə]. *Beer* [biə] and *bar* [bɑː] are different.

6 **d.** *To appear* = to come into sight.

7 **c.** We *kick* with our feet. *To touch* = to put a hand or finger on something. The others are not correct English here.

8 **e**

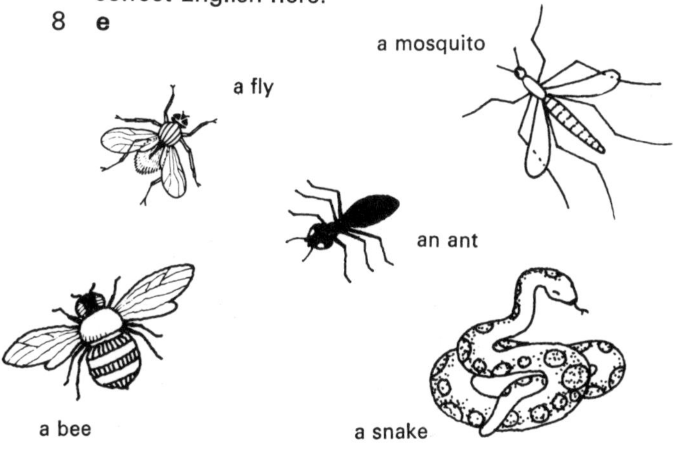

9 **c.** When someone *calls* us on the *telephone*, it *rings* and we *answer* it.
10 **a.** *Purse* [pəːs] and *worse* [wəːs] are the same. Notice: *hours* ['auəz], *course* [kɔːs], *horse* [hɔːs] and *pours* [pɔːz].
11 **d**
12 **a.** We keep coins in *a purse*, but *notes* (paper *money*) in *a wallet*.
13 **e.** *Deep* and *shallow* are used of water; also, deep = (of people) deep-thinking, having many secrets; shallow = (of people) without deep thoughts or feelings. The opposite of *thick* = *thin*. The opposite of *narrow* = *wide*.
14 **b.** We sleep between *sheets*. We dry ourselves on *a towel*. We dry things with *a cloth*. We cover the floor with *a carpet*.
15 **d.** *In good hands* = safe (Don't worry, it's in good hands). *To lend a hand* = to help. *Out of hand* = out of control.
16 **d**
17 **d.** *Nasty* is often used by children for things they do not like.
18 **c.** Notice: *a doctor, a dentist* or *a nurse* can be a man or a woman.
19 **b.** The opposite of *hard* = soft. The opposite of *light* = *dark*. The opposite of *right* = wrong; also, left (right-handed, left-handed).
20 **b.** *A vehicle* = any kind of machine which carries things on land.

Unit three

1 **d.** When *a fire* burns, we usually see *flames*.
2 **d.** *Tiny* = very small. The opposite of *thin* = fat. The opposite of *small* = large. The opposite of *low* = high.
3 **b**

4 **b.** The short name for *Anthony* = Tony. The short name for *Albert* = Bert.

5 **e.** Only birds have *wings* and *a chicken* is a bird.

6 **b.** You climb *onto a horse* when you mount it. You climb *into a plane* when you enter it. Only small children climb *onto a chair*.

7 **d.** *A lamp* and *a light* give out light (an electric lamp or light). We use *a lighter* to light cigarettes and fires. *Lightning* = the strong flash of light in the sky in a thunderstorm.

8 **d.** *Warm* [wɔːm] is different. *Palm* [pɑːm], *calm* [kɑːm], *farm* [fɑːm] and *harm* [hɑːm] are the same.

9 **c.** *Goed* is not an English word.

10 **a.** *Give up your ticket* = Give it to someone (usually to the ticket collector). *He gave up his seat to a lady* = He let the lady have his seat. *The thief gave himself up* = The thief surrendered. *I give up* = I have stopped trying.

11 **a.** *Good fortune!* is old-fashioned. The others are incorrect.

12 **e.** *Taking it* = taking it from someone else. *Picking it* is not good English. Notice: to pick out = to choose. *Holding it* = holding it in her hand, with no movement. *Holding it up* = holding it high.

13 **d.** *A barn* = a large storehouse on a farm. *A haystack* = a large pile of hay (dried grass). *A hut* = a small, wooden building with one room. *A sleeping bag* = a warm bag for sleeping in when camping, outside or in *a tent*.

14 **e.** *Plough* [plau] rhymes with *allow* [əˈlau]. *Follow* [ˈfɔləu], *widow* [ˈwidəu], *fellow* [ˈfeləu] and *rough* [rʌf] do not.

15 **e.** We put our *arms* into *sleeves*. The part of the sleeve which covers the *wrist* is the *cuff*.

16 **d.** The opposite of *death* = life. The opposite of

the *finish* = the start. The opposite of the *close* = the opening; also, the start (at the start of the play, at the close of the play; the opening of a discussion, the close of a discussion).

17 **d.** *Uncertain* = *unsure*.

18 **e**

19 **a.** The *sea* is *water*. A very small amount of water is *a drop*. We *wash* in water.

20 **c.** We never say: He is *hearing the radio*. When you hear a radio, its sound reaches your ears, often from a distance. When you *listen to the radio*, you pay attention to the sound, usually close to it. *Earing the radio* is not English. *Attending to the radio* = working on it, mending it.

Unit four

1 **a.** *Chilly* = rather cold.

2 **a**

3 **d.** The correct word is *paid*.

4 **c**

5 **e.** *Birds* are covered in *feathers*. No animals have feathers.

6 **e.** We *read letters*. We put *stamps* on letters before we *post* them.

7 **c.** *A conductor* = the man on a bus who sells the tickets; also, the man who directs an orchestra. *A guide* = a person who leads people on foot (a mountain guide, a museum guide). *A chauffeur* = a person who is paid to drive a private car. *A driver* = a person who is in control of a car, bus, train, etc (never a plane).

8 **e.** *To persuade* = gently to make someone do something, usually by talking. *To encourage* = to help someone to do something, usually by talking.

9 **a.** *To remove* = to take away, the opposite of to

put. The opposite of *to take out* = to put in. The opposite of *to lower* = to raise. The opposite of *to shut* = to open.

10 **d.** *Leather* is usually brown. *Flowerpots* are usually red. *Cheese* is usually white, yellow, red or even blue. The *sky* is usually blue. We often say the sky is grey, but we really mean the clouds are grey.

11 **c.** Small children sometimes call *a train*, a puffer or a choo-choo.

12 **a.** *Shout* [ʃaut] is different. *Coat* [kəut], *wrote* [rəut], *boat* [bəut] and *note* [nəut] are the same.

13 **d.** The opposite of *happy* = *sad*. Notice: a *happy* person, but we never say a *glad* person. *Miserable* = unhappy. *Funny* = amusing; also, odd or strange. We feel *comfortable* when we sit in a soft armchair.

14 **d**

15 **b.** This is the most usual order.

16 **c**

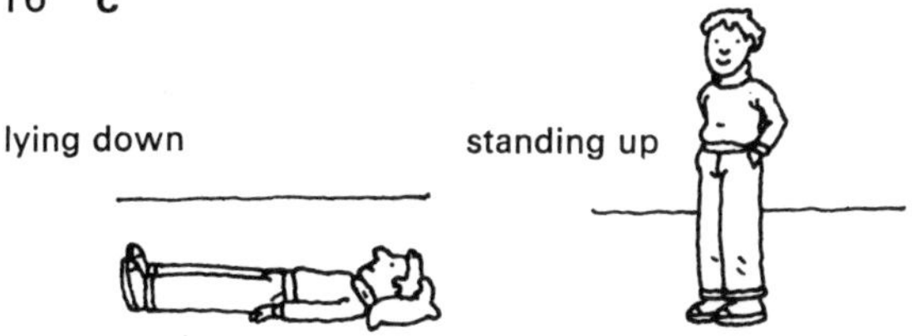

17 **c.** *Unworkable* = impossible (unworkable ideas or plans, but not watches). *Without work* = without a job. *Hard-working* = working very hard (a hard-working man).

18 **b.**

19 **d.** *Practice* ['præktis] has a different sound from *ice* [ais], *mice* [mais], *rice* [rais] and *twice* [twais].

20 **a.** The *sun* shines by *day*: the *moon* shines by *night*.

Unit five

1 **d.** *A building* is made of bricks, stone, wood, etc. *A tent* is made of cloth and is used for camping. We can put up and take down a tent easily.

2 **b.** *Fire burns* things, making *smoke* and *heat*.

3 **e.** The others are not good English.

4 **a.** *Unmoving* = *still*. *Quiet* = without noise, peaceful. *Quick* = *fast*.

5 **d.** *A seat* = something to sit on.

a chair

a sofa or settee

a stool

6 **a.** We have *fingers* on our *hands* and *toes* on our *feet*. Each hand has four fingers and *a thumb*.

7 **e**

8 **a.** *Daffodils* flower in the spring in Britain.

a daffodil

9 **b.** *A mechanic* works with machines, often with motor cars.

10 **d.** We wear collars round the *neck*, bracelets round the *arm* or *wrist*, and people used to wear garters round the *leg* to hold up stockings.

11 **e.** *Counting* and *adding numbers* is part of *arithmetic*. *An adder* = a snake.

12 **c.** *A fence* = *a wall*, usually made of wood, placed round a garden or a field. *An entrance* = a way in (*doors* and *gates* are entrances).

13 **c.** *Bored* and *board* are the same [bɔːd]. *Boat* [bəut] and *bought* [bɔːt] are different.

14 **c.** *Expensive* = dear, costing a lot of money.

15 **e.** The opposite of the *front* = the back.

16 **d.** *A black look* = an angry look. *A black book* = a book where you write the names of people you don't like. *A blacklist* = a list of people you don't like. (We often talk about a black book and a blacklist as a joke.) *A black pudding* = a kind of sausage, made of blood. *A blackboard* = a board in a classroom for writing on with chalk.

17 **e.** *A clearing* = an open space in a wood. We do not say the air is *cleared*. (A table is cleared when we take things off it at the end of a meal.) *A clearance* = making something clear or tidy; also, a clear space. The opposite of *clear* = *unclear*.

18 **a.** *Bead* [biːd] is different. *Said* [sed], *head* [hed], *dead* [ded] and *bread* [bred] are the same.

19 **c.** *A lighter* sets something alight (a cigarette lighter, a fire lighter). *Stop lights* = the red lights at the back of a car which go on when it is stopping. *Car lights* = the lights on a car.

20 **e.** *Air* has no weight.

Unit six

1 **b**

2 **d.** *Flour* and *flower* are the same [ˈflauə]. *Floor* [flɔː], *flew* [fluː], *flow* [fləu] and *flier* [ˈflaiə] are different.

3 **b.** When *buttons* and *apples drop off*, they fall. *Drop me off at the corner* = Let me get out of the car at the corner. *Umbrella sales drop off* = Umbrella sales get less.

4 **e.** The opposite of *few* = many. The opposite of *less* = more. The opposite of *little* = much.

5 **d.** *Taking it to them* = carrying it to them. *Taking it by them* = taking it near them. *Taking it from them* = taking it out of their hands. *Taking it with them* = helping them to take it.

6 **e.** *A paper* = a newspaper. *A packet* = a strong *paper bag* (a packet of tea, sugar). *A parcel* = something wrapped up in string and paper.

7 **d.** We *play music* on *a piano* by pressing the *keys*.

8 **b**

a cup

a dish

a jar

a glass

9 **d.** *Lively* = active, full of life. *Alive* = *living*. *Liveliness* = being lively.

10 **d.** The *thigh* = the leg from the knee upwards.

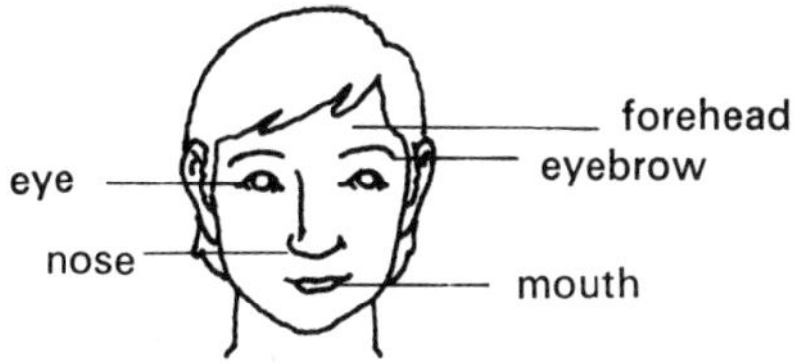

11 **b.** *An artist* works in a studio. *A tobacconist* sells tobacco. *A barber* cuts men's hair. *A grocer* sells tea, flour, biscuits, and many kinds of food. *A butcher* sells meat.

12 **d**

13 **b**

a ladybird

a beetle

a lizard

a worm

14 **e.** The correct sentence is: *They have drunk their tea.*

15 **d.** *Stew* = meat and vegetables cooked slowly in liquid. *A joint* = a large piece of meat, usually with a bone in it. *A chop* = a slice of meat from an animal's ribs. *Mince* = meat cut into tiny pieces by a machine. *Sausages* = minced meat, etc, stuffed into a skin.

16 **c.** *Hired* [ˈhaɪəd] is different. *Stirred* [stəːd], *bird* [bəːd], *word* [wəːd] and *heard* [həːd] have the same sound.

17 **e.** *Humans wear clothes* on their *bodies*.

18 **b**

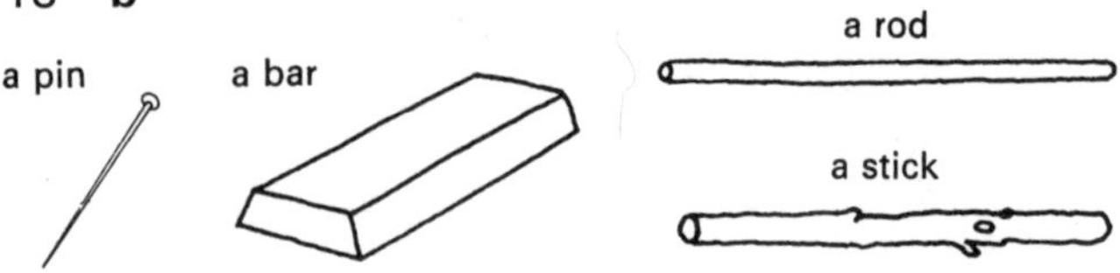

19 **b.** We *listen* with our ears. We *watch, look, see* and *stare* with our eyes.

20 **c**

Unit seven

1 **b.** (*Phone* = telephone.) We go into *a phone box* to make *a phone call*. Sometimes we ask the *operator* to get the number for us. *A directory* = a large book with people's names, addresses and phone numbers in it.

2 **c.** *Rope* is the thickest and strongest. We use *cotton* or *thread* for sewing. We use *string* or *cord* to tie up parcels.

3 **b.** All the others mean the same thing.

4 **c**

5 **a.** *Day* [dei] and *grey* [grei] have the same sound. *Key* [ki:], *quay* [ki:], *free* [fri:] and *dye* [dai] do not.

6 **e.** *I accepted it* = I agreed to have it. *I received it* = someone sent it or gave it to me. *I acquired it* = I got it, but I'm not saying how. *I gained it* = I did something for it.

7 **b.** *A timetable* shows the times of trains, buses or lessons in school. *A date* gives the day, month and year (Today's date is 1 February 1980). *A notice* = information written and put up on a wall for everyone to see. *A diary* = a small pocket book we write in every day.

8 **a.** *Wallpaper* = paper for decorating walls.

9 **c**

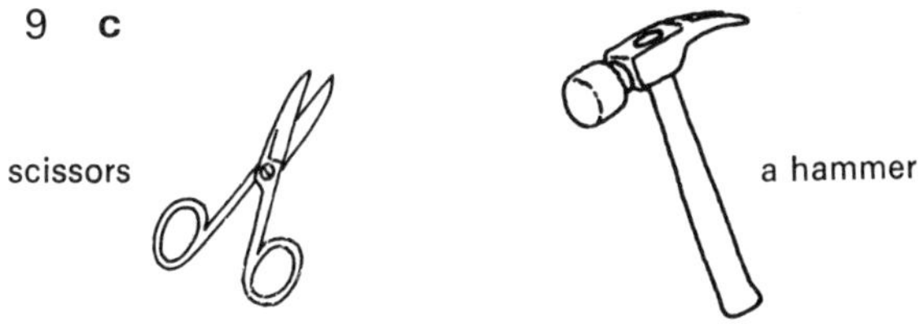

10 **d**

11 **d.** All the others are shapes.

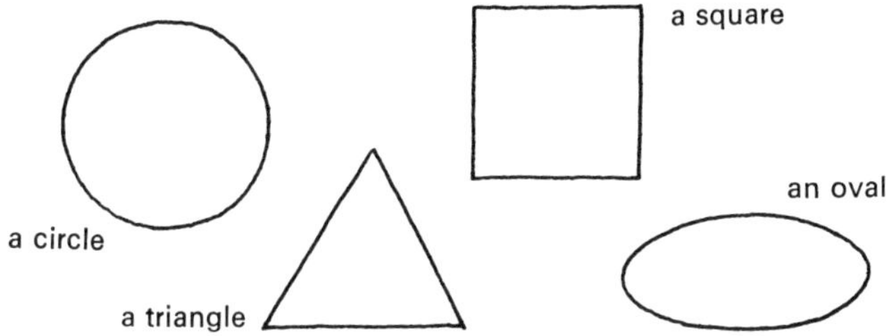

12 **a.** *A beak* = the hard, sharp part of a bird's mouth.

13 **e.** The others are not correct here. The boy is *throwing* the ball.

14 **e.** The correct word is: *cutting*.

15 **d.** The opposite of *nice* = nasty.

16 **b.** *Shall* [ʃæl] is different. *All* [ɔːl], *tall* [tɔːl], *call* [kɔːl] and *hall* [hɔːl] are the same.

17 **e**

18 **a.** *A businessman* works in *an office*; he often attends *meetings* and writes *reports*.

19 **a.** *Sheets, pages* and *bills* are pieces of paper, but not parts of a tree. *A trunk* = the thickest part of a tree.

20 **b.** *Putting your heads together* = thinking together and sharing ideas. *Losing your head* = getting afraid and doing foolish things. *Coming to a head* = coming to a crisis or climax. *Biting someone's head off* = speaking very fiercely to him.

Unit eight

1 **d.** *A slipper* = a light, comfortable *shoe* for the house. *A boot* = a heavy shoe which covers the ankle. We wear *socks* on our feet, inside shoes.
2 **e.** *To close* = *to shut* (opposite of *to open*). The opposite of *to break* = to mend.
3 **b.** *An ocean* = a large *sea* (the Atlantic Ocean, the Red Sea). *A stream* = a small *river. A lake* = a stretch of fresh water.
4 **b.** *A foster mother* = a woman who acts as a mother for another woman's child. If your father marries a second wife, she is your *stepmother*.
5 **b.** *To trouble* = to worry someone. *To chase* = to run after. *To frighten* = to make afraid.
6 **a**

a beret

7 **c.** We carry *cigarettes* in a cigarette case or in their packet, and *tobacco* in a pouch.
8 **b.** *Clocks* tell us the *time*: their *hands* point to the *hours*.
9 **c.** *Skiing* = going on skis. *Sliding* = moving on a slide or a slippery surface. *Slipping* = moving out of control and often falling.

skis

10 **a.** *Having a change of heart* = changing your feelings. *Breaking your heart* = feeling very,

very sad. *Having your heart in your mouth* = being very frightened. *Taking heart* = becoming brave.

11 **b.** *A score* = 20. *A pair* = 2. *A gross* = 144. *A century* = 100 (years).

12 **b**

13 **d.** The others are not good English.

14 **d.** *Fair* and *fare* sound the same [fɛə]. *Fire* [ˈfaiə], *fir* [fəː], *far* [fɑː] and *fear* [fiə] are different.

15 **d.** Trains, planes and buses *arrive* and *depart*. The opposite of *to come* = *to go*.

16 **b.** *To kneel* = to rest on the knees. We *bend* our knees when we kneel. *To knee* = (unusual) to hit with the knee.

17 **d.** *Were* [wəː] has a different sound from *their, there, they're* [ðɛə] and *where* [wɛə].

18 **b.** *Marryed* is not an English word.

19 **c.** *Usherettes* show you to your seat *in a cinema*. Air hostesses work *in aeroplanes*; stewardesses *on ships*; guides *in museums* and porters *in stations*.

20 **b.** When you have *a pain* in your arm, your arm is *painful* and you are *in pain*. *Pained* = troubled (to have a pained expression on your face). *Paining* is not an English word.

Unit nine

1 **a.** *To discover* = to find out (He can't discover my age). The opposite of *to find* = to lose.

2 **a.** The correct sentence is: *They go by themselves.*

3 **a.** Amount tells us *how much*. Quantity tells us *how many*. Length tells us *how long*. Distance tells us *how far*.

4 **b.** We wear *a watch* on our wrist to tell the time. *Spectators* = people who are watching

something, sports, for example. *A spectacle* = something striking and unusual to see. Notice: spectacles = (old-fashioned) *glasses*. *A glass* = something to drink from, made of glass.

5 **b.** All *birds* and some *brushes* have *feathers*. Birds, *aeroplanes*, *animals* and *coats* can have *tails*. Aeroplanes and birds have *wings*.

6 **e.** *Wool* [wul] has a different sound from *cool* [ku:l], *school* [sku:l], *fool* [fu:l] and *you'll* [ju:l].

7 **e.** *Blew* = did blow (the wind blew; he blew his trumpet). Blue is a colour.

8 **c.** We usually *drop* things (to drop a plate). Things drop (his voice dropped) and sometimes people drop (he dropped dead), but dropping is wrong here. *To descend* = *to go down* (a mountain, stairs, etc).

9 **d.** The short name for *Christine* = Chris.

10 **d**

11 **b.** When we *whisper*, *sing* or have *a conversation*, we use our *voices*.

12 **d.** The opposite of *to sell* = to buy. The opposite of *to bring* = to take away.

13 **e.** The others are not correct.

14 **b**

15 **b.** *Gaze* [geiz] rhymes with *praise* [preiz]. *Face* [feis], *prize* [praiz], *prise* [praiz] and *price* [prais] do not.

16 **d.** We *play* musical instruments, e.g. *trumpets*. We take, make and watch *films*. We watch *television*. We listen to *a radio*. We use *a hammer*.

17 **d.** *A heater* gives out heat. Planes and helicopters = *aircraft*. *A cooler* = a container to keep things cool (a butter cooler). *Propellers* drive boats and smaller aeroplanes.

18 **e.** *To call* = to shout. *To add* = to join one thing to another (when you add 2 to 3, you

get 5). *To consist of* = to be made of, to contain (a class consisting of eight boys and twelve girls). *To insist* = to say very strongly. Notice: to aid = *to help*.

19 **d.** *A piece* and *a bit* are not exact amounts. When something is divided into two equal pieces, one of them is *a half*. *Small* = little.

20 **b.** We *wear hats* on our *head*. A hat must be the correct *size*.

Unit ten

1 **a.** *An announcer* = a man or woman who makes announcements (a television or radio announcer; a station announcer who gives the times of trains).

2 **d.** The opposite of *to buy* = *to sell*.

3 **e.** There is no word *thoughtish*: the correct word is *thoughtful*.

4 **b.** *Intelligent* = *clever*. The opposite of clever = *foolish*.

5 **e.** We *swim* in *water* which is *wet*. *A pool* = a small stretch of water.

6 **e.** *Love* [lʌv] has the same sound as *above* [əˈbʌv]. *Move* [mu:v], *stove* [stəuv], *drove* [drəuv] and *wove* [wəuv] are different.

7 **c.** We *mend socks* with a needle.

8 **e.** *A dam* = a very big wall across a river to keep water back. *A shutter* = a wooden cover outside a window.

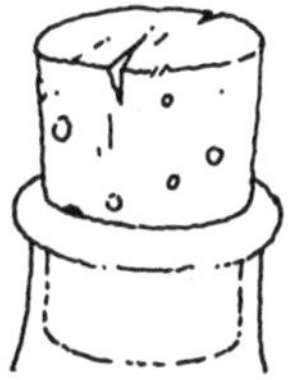

a cork

9 **b.** The *blade* is the *sharp* part of *a knife*, which *cuts*.
10 **e.** Mutton comes from *a sheep*, horse-meat from *a horse*, pork from *a pig*. In Britain people don't eat horse-meat.
11 **e**
12 **c.** All the others are not good English.
13 **c.** Some children say Dad. Nobody says Pa or Papa today. The names for *a mother* = Mummy or Mum.
14 **e.** We *take up* an idea, a sport. *To take away* = to remove. *To take on* = to agree to do something (to take on extra work). *To take above* is not good English.
15 **d.** *Also* is wrong in this position. The correct sentence is: *He also does not like eggs.*
16 **b.** *To know* = to be *certain* or *sure*. The opposite of sure = *unsure*. The opposite of certain = *uncertain*.
17 **c.** All the others are not good English.
18 **e.** *A waiter* brings us *food to eat* in *a restaurant*.
19 **b.** The opposite of *incorrect* = correct. The opposite of *wrong* = right. The opposite of *faithful* = unfaithful.
20 **d.** *Wheels* and *records* are always round. *Balls* and *tins* usually are, although a rugby ball is oval.

Unit eleven

1 **c.** *Raised* [reizd] has a different sound from the others: *placed* [pleist], *waste* [weist], *raced* [reist] and *waist* [weist].
2 **b.** *Looking for her watch* = trying to find where her watch is. The others are not good English.
3 **e.** The other short names are Tom (*Thomas*), Terry (*Terence*), Fred (*Frederick*) and Bill (*William*).

4 **d.** We only *catch* illnesses when we get them from another person.

5 **d.** The children's name for *a horse* = a gee-gee; *a cow* = a moo-cow.

6 **a.** *Drinking, washing, sailing* and *floating* all have something to do with water.

7 **d.** Some special cinemas are called film theatres, but this is unusual. *Acts* and *scenes* are parts of *plays*.

8 **e.** In Britain, *pupils* go to school to have lessons from *teachers*. *Students* go to college or university and have lectures from lecturers. *A scholar* = (old-fashioned) a schoolchild; also, a clever person who knows a lot. *A learner* = someone who is learning (a learner driver).

9 **a.** A *barber's* shop is for men only. A hairdresser's (shop) may be for men or women.

10 **e.** *Would* and *wood* are the same [wud]. *Word* [wəːd] and *world* [wəːld] are different.

11 **e**

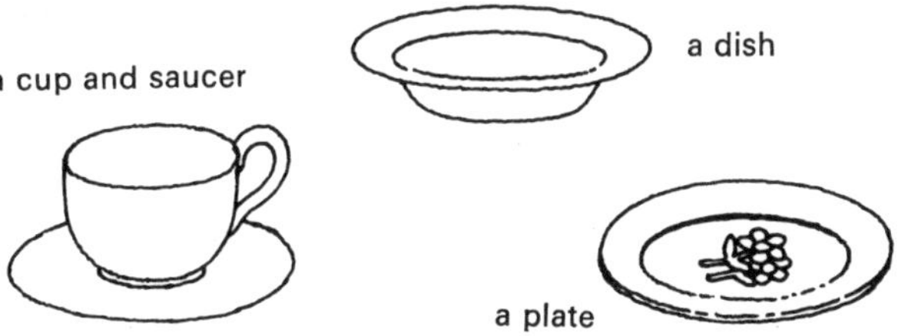

12 **b.** *Fast* = *quick*. *Silent* = without noise. *Rapid* = quick (a rapid movement; never a rapid man).

13 **a.** Notice: He was fast asleep = He was sleeping deeply.

14 **a.** This is not good English. The others all mean the same thing.

15 **e.** You ride *on a bicycle*. We also ride on *a train*, on *a bus* and on *a plane*.

16 **e.** *A fountain* = water sent up into the air. *A drop of water* = the smallest amount of water.
17 **c.** We *draw curtains to cover a window.*
18 **d.** *A pair* = two things the same (a pair of shoes). *A couple* = two (a couple of days, a married couple). *A dozen* = twelve. *A twin* = someone born at the same time as another person, to the same mother.
19 **e.** The opposite of *under* = *over.*
20 **c.** *A sailor* works on a ship. *A builder* works on a building site. *A headmistress* works in a school. *A salesman* works in a shop or a showroom.

Unit twelve

1 **a.** *Honey* is often eaten on bread and butter.

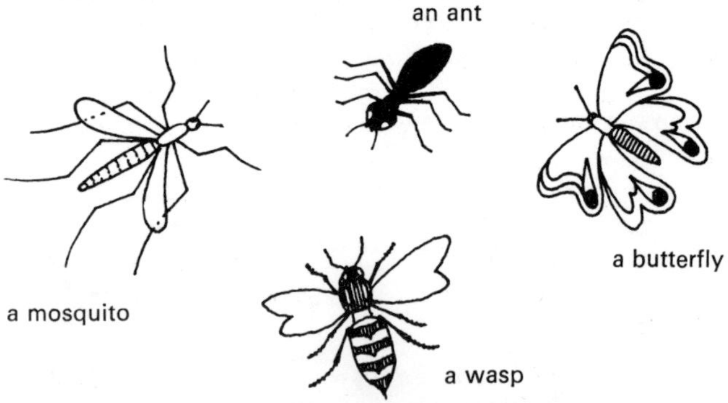

2 **b.** *With a plane* = taking a plane with him! The others are not good English.
3 **a.** Your *nephew* and *niece* = the *son* and *daughter* of your brother or *sister.* You are the uncle or *aunt* of your nephews and nieces.
4 **e.** *An assistant* in *a shop sells* things to *customers.*

5 **e.** All the others = in a little time.
6 **b.** Scotland is *a country*. *A field* = an open piece of ground where food is grown (a cornfield, etc). London is *a city*. *Towns* are smaller than cities. *Villages* are smaller than towns.
7 **e.** *Lions* can kill people.

a lion

8 **a.** He is using a saw to cut it: he is *sawing* it. *To split* wood = *to break* it open from end to end.
9 **b**
10 **d.** *An officer* = someone who has a job of authority (a police officer). *An office* = a room where people work at desks; also, a high public position (the office of Prime Minister). *Official* = to do with people in high public positions; formal. The opposite of official = *unofficial.*
11 **b.** *Broad* [brɔːd] has a different sound from *showed* [ʃəud], *rowed* [rəud], *road* [rəud] and *toad* [təud].
12 **e.** *Pots and pans* = (a fixed phrase) saucepans. Notice: pots of money = very rich.
13 **b**

a basket

a box

a case

a nest

14 **b.** The opposite of *ancient* = modern. *Worn out* = old and no longer useful. *Adult* = fully grown. The opposite of *old* = *young* (for living things).

15 **b.** *Dates* grow on date-palms.

a palm tree

16 **a.** When *a shower* of *rain falls*, we need to wear *a mackintosh* (a mac).

17 **e.** *On the move* = moving. *Making a move* = starting to move. *Moving in* = taking your things into a new place to live. *Moving up* = moving along (making room on a seat for someone else).

18 **c**

19 **a.** All the others are not English words.

20 **a.** *Evening* = the early part of the night.

Unit thirteen

1 **e.** *Fur* = the soft coat of animals. All the others are hard.

2 **d.** We play *badminton* with a shuttlecock.

a shuttlecock

3 **b.** Notice: I am washing my hands, you are washing your hair, etc.

4 **b.** *A doctor* meets his patients in his *surgery*.

5 **a.** *A watch* tells the time. *Watchful* = not sleeping, on the look-out. *Unwatched* = with no one watching. *A watcher* = someone who watches (a bird-watcher).

6 **e**

7 **d.** *A wedding* takes place in *church* when *a bride* and bridegroom are *married.*

8 **d.** *Spot* [spɔt] is different from *thought* [θɔːt], *court* [kɔːt], *ought* [ɔːt] and *sport* [spɔːt].

9 **a.** The opposite of *here* = there. *Nearly* = almost. *Closed* = shut.

10 **a.** *To regard* = to think of (I regard you as my best friend); also (uncommon), to look hard at. *To watch* = to pay attention to.

11 **d.** A greengrocer sells *fruit* and *vegetables.*

12 **e**

13 **b**

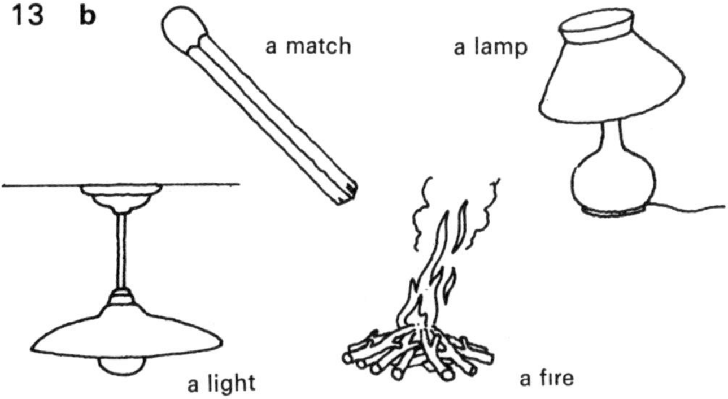

14 **d.** Women wear *dresses. Your home* = where you live. *Your house* = the building you live in.

15 **a.** *Scent* and *sent* sound the same [sent]. Notice: *cent* [sent]. *Cant* [kænt], *scant* [skænt], *saint* [seint] and *send* [send] are different.

16 **a.** When we *sing songs* we are using our *voices* to make *music.*

17 **a.** *A crayon* = a coloured pencil.

18 **c.** The opposite of *high* = low. The opposite of *closed* and *shut* = open. The opposite of *filled* = emptied.

19 **d.** *A biscuit* = a small, flat, dry cake. We don't eat *paper* or *plastic*. We drink *beer* and *whisky*.

20 **b.** *To beat time* = to wave or tap the hand in time to music. *On time* = not late. *In no time* = at once, immediately. *To keep good time* = (of a clock) to be accurate, not losing or gaining time.

Unit fourteen

1 **e.** *Tears* are the drops of water which come into our *eyes* when we *cry* because we are *sad*.

2 **d.** *Knight* and *night* sound the same [nait]. *Neat* [ni:t] and *knit* [nit] are different.

3 **b**

a bucket

a bottle

a bowl

4 **d.** The correct word is: *slept*.

5 **e.** *Fire* burns. *Coal* burns on fires, but is not hot otherwise.

6 **c.** *Pork* = the meat of *a pig*. *Mutton* = the meat of *a sheep*. *Beef* = the meat of *a cow*. Venison = the meat of *a deer*. Veal = the meat of *a calf* (a young cow).

7 **e.** *A disc* = something round, flat and thin. *A buckle* = a fastener on a belt or shoe. *A fastener* = something that fastens (a zip fastener).

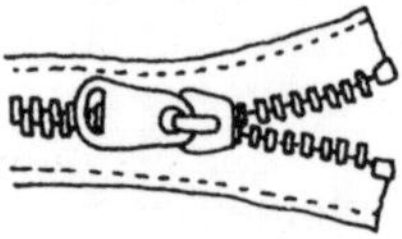

a zip

8 **b.** *Iron* is the commonest metal.
9 **c.** Height tells us *how high*. Temperature tells us *how cold*. Frequency tells us *how often*. Size tells us *how big*.
10 **d.** All the other words = *two*. *Twice* = two times. *A pair* = two the same. *Twins* = two born at the same time to the same mother.
11 **e.** *A night club* = a place of entertainment where people drink, dance, listen to singers, etc. *A nurse* works in a hospital. *A patient* = a sick person in hospital. *Ill* = not well, sick. Sick people take *medicine* to get better.
12 **a.** The correct sentence is: *His leg looked painful.*
13 **b.** Children *colour* pictures in books with coloured pencils. We *brush* our hair, teeth or our clothes.
14 **a.** The opposite of *dark* = light. The opposite of *untidy* = tidy. The opposite of *black* = white. The opposite of *bad* = good.
15 **a**
16 **b**
17 **a.** All the others are not good English.
18 **c.** *A can* is now a usual English word for *a tin* (a can of beer, a can of soup). Twenty years ago English people said *tin* where Americans said *can*.
19 **c.** *A season* = one of spring, summer, autumn or winter.
20 **e.** The opposite of *out* = in. The opposite of *over* = *under*.

Unit fifteen

1 **c.** *A boss* = (slang) a chief, an employer. The opposite of *a slave* = a master. *A neighbour* = someone who lives or sits near you. *A pal* = (informal) a friend.

2 **e**

3 **e.** The *eye socket* = the hole in which the eye fits. The *eyeball* = the whole eye (the white and coloured parts).

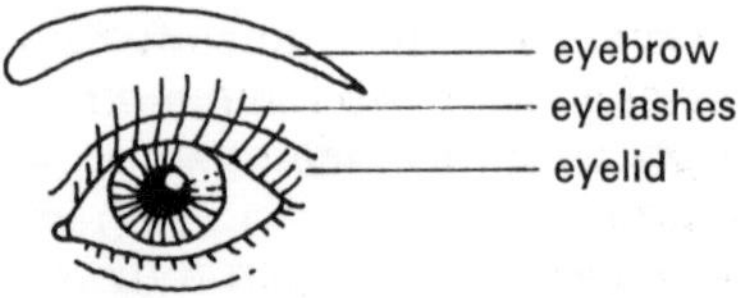

4 **a.** *A scarf* = a piece of material to wear round the neck. *A paw* = the foot of *an animal* (a dog, cat, rabbit). Some animals (horses, lions) have *a mane* on their heads. We often call an animal's fur, its *coat*.

5 **e.** *Flow* [fləu] and *hoe* [həu] have the same sound. *Bough* [bau], *through* [θru:], *thaw* [θɔ:] and *zoo* [zu:] are different.

6 **b.** We wear *a belt* round our waist. *Stockings* are longer than *socks*. *Boots* are heavier than *shoes*.

7 **a.** *Teachers* write on the *blackboard* when they teach *pupils* in the *classroom*. *A prison* = a building where law-breakers are kept.

8 **b.** *To dive* = to go down head first, usually into water.

9 **a.** When you have the same ideas as someone, you *agree* with him. You are in *agreement*. *Disagreeable* = unpleasant. When you make an agreement, something is *agreed*.

10 **c.** The edge of *a river* = *a bank*. The edge of the *sea* = the *shore*. The shore is also the edge of the *land*. Sometimes there are *shells* and *sand* on the shore.

11 **b.** The correct sentence is: *He found happiness.*

12 **e**

13 **b.** The opposite of *to send* = to receive (letters, messages). The opposite of *to bring* = to take away. *To tow* = to pull along behind (to tow a car to a garage).

14 **e.** *A playground* = a special place for children to play in safety (usually at school). *A playroom* = a special room for children to play in. *A plaything* = a toy. The others are not usual English phrases.

15 **a.** *To turn a corner* = to go round a corner.

16 **b.** *Worried* [ˈwʌrid] has a different sound from *ride* [raid], *died* [daid], *hide* [haid] and *inside* [inˈsaid].

17 **c.** *Helpish* is not an English word. The others are all true.

18 **b.** *A notice* = written information in a public place. *Signs* also give information and instructions (road signs).

19 **c.** *A cashier* works with money in *a bank* or shop.

20 **a.** People very often eat slices of *bread* with *butter* on them, especially at tea-time.

Ihr Testergebnis

Unit one	
Unit two	
Unit three	
Unit four	
Unit five	
Unit six	
Unit seven	
Unit eight	
Unit nine	
Unit ten	
Unit eleven	
Unit twelve	
Unit thirteen	
Unit fourteen	
Unit fifteen	
GESAMT	

Wie geht es weiter?

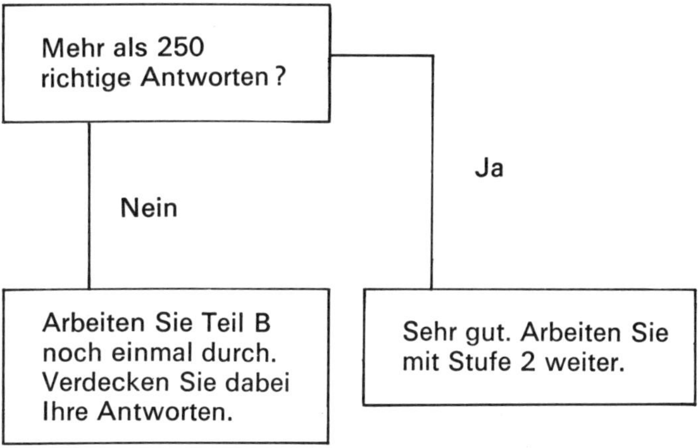

Inhalt